"Andie, we're going to figure this out. I don't k."

She nodded. "We ___ ___ away, but Ryder ___ ___ er to meet his gaze. ___ ___ curved into something delicious.

That smile was her downfall. She should turn away. But his eyes were dark and tempting, like chocolate.

"We should definitely go," she whispered.

"I know, but there's one thing we need to do before we leave."

His lips touched hers in a gesture that was sweet and disarming. Then he paused and rested his forehead against hers.

"We shouldn't have gone there," Andie said.

"Andie, at least give me a chance to figure this all out before you give up on me."

"I've never given up on you. But I have to make the right decisions, now more than ever."

"And you think turning down my proposal was the right decision?"

"Yeah. It was sweet of you, but it was spur-of-the-moment and this is something that we should take time to think about."

Spur-of-the-moment was definitely a bad idea.

Books by Brenda Minton

Love Inspired

Trusting Him
His Little Cowgirl
A Cowboy's Heart
The Cowboy Next Door
Rekindled Hearts
Blessings of the Season
  "The Christmas Letter"
Jenna's Cowboy Hero
The Cowboy's Courtship
The Cowboy's Sweetheart

BRENDA MINTON

started creating stories to entertain herself during hour-long rides on the school bus. In high school she wrote romance novels to entertain her friends. The dream grew and so did her aspirations to become an author. She started with notebooks, handwritten manuscripts and characters that refused to go away until their stories were told. Eventually she put away the pen and paper and got down to business with the computer. The journey took a few years, with some encouragement and rejection along the way—as well as a lot of stubbornness on her part. In 2006 her dream to write for the Steeple Hill Love Inspired line came true. Brenda lives in the rural Ozarks with her husband, three kids and an abundance of cats and dogs. She enjoys a chaotic life that she wouldn't trade for anything—except, on occasion, a beach house in Texas. You can stop by and visit at her Web site, www.brendaminton.net.

The Cowboy's Sweetheart
Brenda Minton

Steeple
Hill®

Published by Steeple Hill Books™

STEEPLE HILL BOOKS

Steeple
Hill®

ISBN-13: 978-0-373-81494-7

THE COWBOY'S SWEETHEART

www.SteepleHill.com

Printed in U.S.A.

Let us therefore come boldly unto the throne
of grace, that we may obtain mercy,
and find grace to help in time of need.

Dedicated to the readers, for the wonderful
e-mails, letters and prayers.

To the editors at Steeple Hill, for the opportunity
to write the books that I love and for
encouragement along the way.
You're the best.

To my family, for all of the love and support
you've given me.

To God, for giving me the desires of my heart.

Chapter One

You have to cowboy up, Andie. Get back on, even if it hurts.

Andie Forester swiped a finger under her eyes and took in a deep breath. She hit the control on the steering wheel to turn down the radio, because it was the fault of Brooks & Dunn and that song of theirs that she was crying. "Cowgirls Don't Cry."

Whatever.

The song made her think of her dad pulling her to her feet after a horse had thrown her. She remembered her world when he was no longer in it. And the song reminded her how it felt to have a sister so perfect the world couldn't love her enough.

Andie even loved Alyson. How could she not? Alyson had come to Dawson and back into her life, soft smiles and sunshine after a twenty-five-year separation. Andie was home just in time to help her sister prepare for her wedding to Jason Bradshaw. A beautiful wedding, with the perfect flowers, the perfect dress.

At the moment Andie wanted to throw up because she was Andie Forester and she didn't think like that. She didn't think sunshine and lace. She thought leather boots and saddles. She thought hard and tough. She was a tomboy. She knew how to hang with the crowd, with cowboys and stock contractors, and guys from Dawson, Oklahoma.

But her dad had been wrong. Brooks & Dunn were wrong. Sometimes cowgirls did cry. Sometimes, on a dusty road in Oklahoma when there wasn't anyone around to see, cowgirls sobbed like little girls in pigtails.

Sometimes, when her best friend had hurt her in a way she had never thought he could, a cowgirl cried.

But she'd get it out of her system before she got to Dawson, and she'd be fine. Ryder Johnson wasn't going to get to her, not again.

That was another thing about Foresters. They learned from their mistakes. She shouldn't have made this mistake in the first place. That's what really got to her.

She downshifted as she drove through the tiny town of Dawson, all three businesses and twenty or so houses. The trailer hooked to her truck jerked a little and she glanced in the rearview mirror, smiling because even Dusty was glad to be home. The dusty gold of his nose was sticking out of the side window, his lips curled a little as he sniffed the familiar scents in the air.

Home was where people knew her. Yeah, they knew her secrets, they knew her most embarrassing moments, but people knowing her was good. The folks in Dawson had shaken their heads, sometimes laughed at her antics, but they'd always been there for her.

The end of September was a good time to return to Oklahoma. The weather would be cooling off and in a month or so, the leaves would change colors.

She would get back to normal. Home would do that for her.

Andie took in another deep breath, and this time she didn't feel the sting of tears. She was done crying. Her pep talk to herself had worked.

She slowed as she drove past the Mad Cow Café and pretended she wasn't looking for Ryder's truck. But she was. It was an old habit. She consoled herself with that thought. And with another one—his truck wasn't there. Hopefully he was still on the road. She didn't want to run into him, not yet.

They'd both been going in opposite directions as fast as they could, putting distance between them and their big mistake. He'd gone back to riding bulls or steer roping, whatever he was doing this year. She'd taken off for Wyoming and a rodeo event she hadn't wanted to miss. Even her trips home had been planned for the times she knew he'd be gone.

The last time Ryder had seen her, well, she'd done a lot of changing since then. She wasn't ready to talk to him about any of that.

At least Dawson hadn't changed. That was something Andie could count on. Her hometown would always be the safe place to land. Jenny Dawson, the town matriarch whose grandfather had started this little community, would always be in her front yard wearing a floral print housedress, digging in her flower gardens, a wide-brimmed hat shading her face from the Oklahoma sun. Omar Gregs would forever be in the corral outside his big barn, a shovel in hand, and that old dog of his sniffing at a rabbit trail.

And Granny Etta would always be at home, waiting.

She slowed as she drove past the Johnson ranch, past the drive that led to Ryder's house. Her best friend. Her heart clenched, the pain unfamiliar, sinking from her heart to her stomach. He'd never been the one to make her feel that way.

The truck jerked a little, evidence of a rest-less horse that had been in a trailer for too many hours. Andie downshifted as she approached the drive that led to the barn. It felt good to see the yellow Victorian she'd grown up in. It looked just the way it had the last time she was at home. Flowers bloomed profusely out of control. The lavender wicker furniture on the front porch was a sign that all was well in the world.

As she turned into the drive, Andie noticed a big sedan on the other side of the house, parked in the driveway that company used. Company, great.

Etta walked out the front door, waving big.

Andie's grandmother had hair that matched the furniture on the porch, kind of. It was the closest the stylist in Grove could get to lavender. And it clashed something horrible with Etta's tanned skin. A Native American woman with Irish ancestors didn't have the complexion to carry off lavender hair.

But tall and thin, she did have the ability to carry off some wild tie-dyed clothes. The clothing was her own design, her own line, and it sold nationwide.

Andie drove the truck down the drive and parked at the barn. Etta was fast-walking across the lawn, the wind swirling the yellow-and-pink tie-dyed skirt around her long legs.

Andie hopped out of the truck and ran to greet her grandmother. Andie was twenty-eight years old—almost twenty-nine—and a hug had never felt so good. When Etta wrapped strong arms around her and held her tight, it was everything.

It was a bandage on a heart that wasn't broken, more like bruised and confused. She hadn't expected it to take this long to heal.

"Sweetheart, it's been too long. And why that serious face and no smile? Didn't you call and tell me things were good?"

"Things *are* good, Gran."

"Well, now why am I not buying that?"

"I'm not sure." Andie smiled as big as she could and her granny gave her a critical stare before shaking her head.

"Okay, get Dusty Boy out of that trailer and let's go inside. I bet you're hungry."

"I am hungry." Starving. She'd been starving for the past few weeks. She was just sick of truck-stop and hotel-restaurant food. Even when she'd stopped in with friends, it hadn't been the same. Nobody cooked like Etta.

Andie moved the latch on the trailer and stepped inside, easing down the empty half of the trailer to unhook Dusty. He shook his head, glad to be free and then backed out, snorting, his hooves clanging loud on the floor of the trailer.

"Come on, boy, time for you to have a run in the pasture."

"Where'd you stay last week?" Etta was standing outside, shading her face with her hand, blocking the glare of the setting sun.

Andie held tight to the lead rope, giving Dusty a minute to calm down. His head was up and his ears alert as he snorted and pawed the ground, eager to be back in the pasture with the other horses.

"I was at Joy and Bob's."

"You were in Kansas? Why didn't you just come on home?"

Because she didn't want to face Ryder and she'd heard he might be home. She'd planned her timing lately so that she was home when he wasn't. But how did she explain that to Etta?

She shrugged, "I was looking at a mare they have for sale."

Not a lie.

The roar of a truck coming down the road caught their attention. Dusty dipped his head to pull at a bite of clover, but he looked up, golden ears perked, twisting like radar as he tuned into the noises around him. He snorted and grabbed another mouthful of grass. Andie pulled on the lead rope and his head came up.

The truck slowed at their driveway. Etta beamed. "Well, there's that Ryder Johnson. He's been down here three times in the past week. He says he's checking on me, but I think he misses his running buddy."

"I'm sure. If he missed me that much..." He would have called. Two months, he could have called. He hadn't.

Etta shot her a look, eyes narrowing. "What's going on with you two kids?"

"Well, first of all, we're not kids. Second, he needs to grow up."

"Oh, so that's the way the wind blows."

"This might be Oklahoma, but the wind isn't blowing, Etta." Andie turned toward the barn, Dusty at her side. He rubbed his big head on her arm and she pushed him back. "Bad manners, Dusty."

"Where are you going?" Etta hurried to catch up.

"To put my horse up."

"Well, I guess I'll make tea."

Tea was Etta's cure for everything.

"Don't invite him for tea, Etta. I'll take care of this, but he doesn't need to hang out here."

"Nonsense." And Etta stormed off, like a wise grandmother who had dealt with her share of love-sick kids. Andie shook her head and unhooked the gate. She wasn't lovesick.

She was mad at herself. And mad at Ryder.

"Off you go, Dusty. Eat some green grass and I'll be back later."

She watched, smiling as her horse made a dash around the field, bucked a few times and then found a place to roll on his back. And then she couldn't put it off any longer. She turned, and there he was, walking toward her, his hat low over his eyes. She didn't need to see those eyes. Brown, long dark lashes. He had a dimple in his chin and a mouth that flashed white teeth when he smiled. He had rough hands that could hold a woman tight and a voice that sounded raspy and smooth, all at the same time.

Those were things she had just learned about him, eight weeks ago. Before that he'd had a voice that teased and hands that held hers tight when they climbed fences or arm wrestled. He had been the person she told her secrets to and shared her fears with.

More than anything she was mad that he couldn't be that person right now. Instead, he was the person she needed to talk about.

He was tall, a cowboy who wore faded jeans, ripped at the knees, and button-down shirts, plaid with pearl buttons. He was her best friend. They'd been friends for twenty-five years, since his family moved to Dawson from Tulsa. His dad had done something right with the stock market. His mom had inherited a chunk of cash.

It hadn't been a perfect life though, and a little over five years ago his parents had died in a car accident.

She'd been there for him.

He'd buried his face into her shoulder and she remembered her fingers on soft, brown hair.

She remembered waking up weeks ago, knowing her life would never be the same. One night, one mistake, and her world had come unraveled.

And then God had hemmed it up again. She'd been running from God longer than she'd been running from Ryder. God had caught her first.

Ryder watched the changing expressions on Andie's face and he wondered what kind of storm he was about to face. Would it be the summer kind that passes over with little damage, or the other kind, the kind that happens when hot air meets cold?

He had a feeling that it was the hot-meets-cold kind. She had gone from something that looked like sad, to pretty close to furious, and now she was smiling. But the coldness in her eyes was still there. She had latched the gate and she was strong again.

She stood next to the barn, looking a lot like she had the last time he'd seen her. She was a country girl, born and raised in Dawson. Her idea of dressing up was changing into a new pair of jeans and boots that weren't scuffed. She was tall, slim, with short blond hair and brilliant blue eyes.

And she had every right to be angry.

He slowed a little, because maybe this wasn't a hornet's nest he wanted to walk into. It was going to get worse when she found out who was in the house waiting for her. She leaned back against the barn, the wind lifting her hair, blowing it around her face.

"Did you forget how to use a phone?" Yep, she was mad. Her voice was a little softer, a little huskier than normal.

"Nope. I just thought I'd give you a few weeks to get over being mad at me," he said.

"I wouldn't have been mad if you had left a note, called, maybe met up with me somewhere."

"I know." He cracked his knuckles and she glared. He took that to mean she wanted more than an easy answer. "I'm not good at relationships."

Understatement. And it was an explanation she didn't need from him. His parents had spent his childhood fighting, drinking and socializing. The ranch here in Dawson had saved him. At least he'd had horses to keep him busy and out from under their feet.

Away from his parents had usually been the best, safest bet for a kid.

He'd had Andie to run with and Etta's house as a safe haven. Right at that moment Andie looked anything but safe. Standing there with her arms wrapped around herself, hugging her middle tight, she looked angry, sad, and about a dozen other female emotions he didn't want to put a name on.

"Relationship? This isn't a relationship, Ryder. This is us. We were friends."

"Oh, come on, we're still friends." He slipped an arm around her shoulder and she slid out of the embrace. "We'll go out tomorrow, maybe drive into Tulsa. It'll be like old times."

"Nope." She walked quickly toward the house. He kept up.

So, the rumors were true. "This is about church, isn't it?"

She stopped abruptly and turned. "No, it isn't about church. You think that going to church would make me mad at you? Don't be an idiot."

"Well isn't that what people do when they feel guilty?" He winked. "They get right with God?"

"Shut up, Ryder."

She took off again, arms swinging, boots stomping on the dry grass.

"We've been friends forever."

"Right." She stopped and when she glanced up, before she could shake the look, he thought she looked hurt.

The way she'd looked hurt when he'd turned eleven and she'd been about ten, but not quite. He'd had a bunch of boys over and she hadn't been invited. He'd told her it was a guys-only party and she'd wanted to be one of the guys, because she was his best friend.

Now he realized that best friends shouldn't be easy to hold or feel soft in a guy's arms. Or at least he thought that was the case. He didn't want to lose someone who had always been there for him. He didn't want to turn her into his mom.

He sure didn't want to be his dad.

He wanted them to stay the way they were, having fun and hanging out. Not growing up, growing angry, growing apart. He didn't want to think about how selfish that sounded, keeping her in his life that way.

"Andie, I didn't plan for this to mess up our friendship."

"Neither of us planned for that. And this isn't about…" She looked away. "This is about you not calling me back."

"Because I didn't know what to say."

"Ryder, you're almost thirty and I've heard you talk to women. You always know what to say."

She looked down, shuffling her feet in the dusty driveway. "But you didn't know what to say to me?"

"I'm sorry." He hadn't known what to say and he still didn't. With other women, he just said what felt right at the moment. And man, he'd had a lot of nasty messages on his answering machine over the years, because he'd said what felt right, not what mattered.

"You don't have to apologize. We're both responsible."

"I know, but we made a promise. I made a promise." A promise to keep boundaries between them. "I don't know what else to say, except I'm sorry."

"You should have called." She had shoved her hands in her front pockets and she stared up at him, forcing his thoughts back to that. That night in Phoenix he'd found her standing behind her trailer, crying because she'd been rejected by her mother. He'd never seen her like that, hurt that way.

He shook his head, chasing off memories that were more than likely going to get him in trouble again.

"Come on, Andie, give me a break. You know me better than anyone. You know that I'm not good at this. You know that we were both there. We both..."

"Stop. I don't want to talk about what we both did. I want to talk to you about us."

Heat crawled up his neck, into his face. "Andie, you sound like a woman."

"I am a woman."

"No." He took off his hat and swiped a hand through his hair. "No, you're not. You're my best friend. You're my roping buddy. You're not like other women. You've never been like other women, getting all caught up in the dating thing and romance."

"I'm still not caught up in those things."

"No, now you're caught up in religion."

"I'm not caught up in anything. This is about faith. And to be honest, I really needed some." She looked away.

"Whatever. I'm just saying, this isn't you."

"It's me. But for a lot of years, I've been trying to be who you wanted me to be. I've done a lot of things to make you feel better about being angry." Her voice was soft and sweet, reminding him of how easy it had been to kiss her. Maybe things had changed—more than he'd realized. Being on the road he'd been able to fool himself into believing that they could go right back to being who they'd always been.

"Go to supper with me at the Mad Cow. I'll buy you a piece of pecan pie." He nudged her shoulder and she nodded. He thought she might say yes.

But then she shook her head. "I'm tired. It was a long trip."

"Yeah, I guess it was. Maybe tomorrow?"

"Tomorrow's Sunday."

"And you're going to church?"

"Yeah, Ryder, I'm going to church."

"Fine, I've got to get home and get things cleaned up before Wyatt gets here."

"Wyatt's coming?"

Ryder pulled his keys out of his pocket. This was something she would have known, before. He would have called her to talk it over with her, to get her opinion. He guessed that was a pretty good clue that he'd been avoiding her, and telling himself a whole pack of lies.

Number one being that nothing had changed.

"Yeah, he's coming home."

And Ryder didn't know how it would work, with him, Wyatt and two little girls all in one big, messy house. The girls needed to be here, though. Ryder knew that. He knew his brother was falling apart without Wendy. Wyatt was caving under the guilt of his wife's death. A year, and he was still falling apart.

"If you need anything." Andie's voice was gentle, so was her hand on his arm.

"Yeah, I know you're here." He smiled down

at her, winking, because he needed to find firm footing. "Gotta run. Let me know if you change your mind about, well, about anything."

About being this new person, this woman that he just didn't get.

"Right, I'll let you know."

The back door opened. He waved at Etta and tried to escape, but she left the back stoop and headed in their direction. And then he remembered why he'd driven down here. Because mad or not, Andie was about to need a friend.

"Don't you want to come in for tea?" Etta had been filling him with tea for years. Tea for colds, tea for his aches and pains, tea to help him sleep when his parents died. He'd turned to something a little stronger for a few years, until he realized that it was doing more than helping him sleep. It had been turning him into his dad.

He glanced at Andie, and she was still clueless. "I can come in for a minute. I have to get my house clean before Wyatt shows up."

Why'd he have to feel so old all of a sudden? Last week he'd still felt young, like he had it all, except responsibility. He had liked it that way.

"When's he going to be here?" Etta stepped a little closer.

"Tomorrow or Monday. I guess I'll have to call Ruby to get my house really clean."

"You'll be fine, Ryder." Etta's eyes were soft, a little damp.

"Yeah, I'm more worried about Wyatt." Ryder didn't want to think about the house and the girls, not all in the same thought.

And then the back door opened again.

Chapter Two

Andie had forgotten about that car in the drive.
She shouldn't have forgotten. It was Ryder's fault
and it would have felt good to tell him that. But
she didn't have time because the woman standing on the back porch was now walking down
the steps. She was nearing fifty and stunningly
beautiful. And she was smiling. Andie hadn't
expected the smile. She wanted this woman to be
cold, to live up to Andie's expectations of her.

A woman that ditched a child couldn't be
warm. She couldn't be loving. Andie replayed
her list of words she used to describe her mother:
cold, unfeeling, hard, selfish.

The list used to be more graphic, but Andie
was working hard on forgiving. She'd started
with the easy "need to forgive" list. She would
forgive Margie Watkins for spreading a rumor
about her. She could forgive Blaine for gum in

her notebook back in the fifth grade. She'd kept her mother on a list by herself, a final project. Saving the most difficult for last.

So now Andie knew that it was true—God had his own timing, reminding her that He was really the one in charge. She had really thought she'd wait a few months to contact Caroline.

"You okay?" Ryder stepped next to her. "I thought I ought to be here for you."

Cowgirls do too cry. They cry when the man they are the angriest with shows up and says something like that. They can cry when they see their mother for the first time in twenty-five years. She nodded in answer to his question and blinked away the tears, because she'd never cried this much in her life and she didn't like it.

She didn't like that her edge was gone.

Was this really the plan, really what God wanted? For her to forgive the person who had hurt her more than anyone else, even more than Ryder when he ignored her phone calls?

If so, it was going to take some time.

"Caroline wanted to see you." Etta's tone was noncommittal and Andie wondered if her mother had been invited or just showed up.

Oh, the wedding. Alyson's wedding.

"Did she?" Andie managed to stand tall. "Or is she here to see Alyson? To help plan the wedding."

It made sense that her mother would show up to help plan Alyson's wedding. She had never shown up for anything that had to do with Andie.

"I'm here to see you." Caroline was close enough to hear, to respond. And she had the nerve to smile like she meant it.

But really? Did she?

"That's good." Andie managed words that she didn't feel. Standing there in the yard, the sun sinking into the western horizon, red and glowing, the sky lavender. The sky matched Etta's hair. At least that lightened the mood.

"I know I should have come sooner." Caroline glanced away, like she, too, had noticed the setting sun. She stared toward the west. "I don't have excuses. I'm just here to say that I'm sorry."

"Really?" Apparently it was the day for apologies. Was it on the calendar—a national holiday?

"We should go in and have that tea." Etta gathered them the way a hen gathered chicks.

"Ryder, you should go." Andie squeezed his hand. "Thank you for being here."

"You're okay?"

"I'm fine. I'll see you at church tomorrow." She said it to watch the look on his face. She knew he wouldn't be there. He'd gone to church when he was a kid, until his dad's little indiscretion.

"That's one thing I can't do for you, Andie." He kissed the top of her head. "I'll see you around."

Why did it have to sound like goodbye, as if they were sixteen and breaking up?

She watched him get in his truck and drive away. And it wasn't what she wanted, not at all. She wanted her best friend there with her, the way he would have been there for her if Phoenix hadn't happened, if they hadn't spent weeks not knowing what to say to each other.

Watching his truck turn out of the driveway and head down the road, she felt shaken, and her stupid heart felt like it was about to have a seizure of some kind.

And her mother was standing in front of her, waiting for her to pull it together. Caroline, her mother. But Etta had been that person to Andie. Etta had been the one who taught her to be a woman. Etta had taught her to put on makeup, and helped her dress for the prom. Etta had held her when she cried.

Caroline had been in some city far away, being a mother to Andie's twin, and to her half siblings. She'd left the less-than-perfect child with the less-than-perfect husband.

Issues. Andie had a lot of issues to deal with. But she wasn't the mess some people thought she should be. She'd had Etta. She'd had a dad who'd done his best. She'd been taught to be strong, to not be a victim. Now those seemed like easy words that didn't undo all of the pain.

"Come on." Etta took her by the hand and led her to the house.

"Of course, tea will make this all better." Andie whispered. As if tea could make getting steamrollered feel any better.

They walked through the back door into the kitchen decorated with needlepoint wall hangings that Andie and Etta had worked on together. They'd never had satellite, and only a few local stations until recently. Winters had been spent reading or doing needlepoint. It hadn't been a bad way to grow up.

"What's going on between you and Ryder?" Etta spooned sugar into the cup of tea she'd just poured. "If I didn't know better, I'd think that was a lover's quarrel."

"We'd have to be in love for that to be the case." Andie leaned in close to her grandmother, loving the way she smelled like rose talcum powder, and the house smelled like vegetables from the garden and pine cleaner.

It was her grandmother's house and it always felt like the safest place in the world.

Even with her mother standing across the counter from her, fidgeting with the cup that Etta had set in front of her it was still that safe place. Caroline looked up and Andie met her gaze.

"Well, it was just a matter of time," Etta whispered as she walked away.

"What did you say?"

"I said, I hope you don't mind sugar in this tea, and do you mind if it has thyme. It's good for you, you know."

"Right."

She sat down at the kitchen island and her granny slid the cup of tea across the counter to her. Etta sat down next to her, moving a plate of cookies between them. Peanut butter, nothing better.

Andie sipped her tea and set the cup down, not feeling at all better, not the way she usually did when she came home.

"I'm surprised to see you." Andie reached for a second cookie. "I'm the reject kid, right? The one you didn't want."

Caroline shuddered and Andie didn't feel better, not the way she'd thought she would feel the sense of satisfaction she'd expected. And now, not so much.

"You're not defective. You're beautiful, smart and talented," Etta spoke up, her voice having a loud edge.

Andie shot her grandmother a look, because they both knew better. She and her father hadn't been good enough for Caroline. He'd been Caroline's one-night stand in college, and he'd married her. A cute country boy from Oklahoma. And reality hadn't been as much fun.

One-night stands didn't work. She sipped her tea and pushed the thought from her mind. Better to focus on Caroline and her father rather than on her own mistakes.

"I'm not the prodigy. I'm the kid who struggled to read." Andie no longer felt like the kid in school who didn't understand what everyone else got with ease. She had been fortunate to have great teachers, people who were willing to help and encourage her. She'd had Etta.

"You have a challenge, not a disability." Etta covered Andie's hand with a hand that was a little crooked with arthritis, but still strong, still soft, still manicured. "She took Alyson. I got to keep you. That wasn't so bad, was it? Being here with me and your dad?"

Caroline spoke up. "It wasn't bad, was it? I mean, I know Etta loves you. Your dad loved you."

"You can't comment. You weren't here." Andie closed her eyes and tried to let go of the sparks of anger that shot from her heart, hot and cold.

"I can comment." Caroline's hand shook as she set her cup on the counter. "I can comment, because I know what I did and why I did it. I couldn't take this life. I couldn't be a cowboy's wife and the mom to two girls. I couldn't be from Dawson."

Andie shook her head, feeling a little sick with guilt, with hurt feelings. "Really, would it have been that hard?"

"I don't know."

Andie finished off the last of her cookie and drained her cup of tea, and she still didn't know what to say to Caroline Anderson—the woman who had never been her mother.

She thought about this two months ago when she'd slipped into a church service held at the rodeo arena after one of the events. She had sat there wondering how to put her life back together. The pieces were in her hands; Alyson, her mother and Ryder.

It was up to her to put it all back together. It was up to her to forgive.

Andie hopped off the stool. "I have to take care of my horse."

And she planned on spending the night in the camper of her horse trailer. It wasn't really running away. She was giving herself space and a little time to think.

Ryder woke up the next morning to the rumble of a truck in his driveway. He peeked out the window as Wyatt jumped out of a rented moving truck and then reached in for the two little girls who resembled their mom.

As he watched them cut across the lawn— Wyatt holding both girls, looking as sad as they looked—Ryder ran a hand through his hair and shook his head. Man, this was a lot of reality to wake up to.

He glanced at the clock on the coffeemaker as he walked through the kitchen. Nearly ten on a Sunday morning. And Etta's old Caddy was going down the road, because it was time for church. And for the first time in years, Andie was in the passenger seat.

Too much reality.

Too many changes. He was nearly thirty and suddenly everything was changing. Andie was going to church and she didn't want to talk to him. Not that he really blamed her.

But he wanted her back, the way it was before. He wanted it to be like it had been before their night in Phoenix, before her trip to the altar and God. Not that he had anything against God. He knew there was one. He'd been to church. He'd heard the sermons. He'd even prayed.

But his parents had gone, too. They'd picked a church in a neighboring town, not Dawson Community Church. And that had just about done him in on religion. His parents, their lifestyle and then the day in church when someone brought his dad forward. Man, he could still remember that day, the looks people had given him, the way it had felt to hear what his dad had done.

And he remembered the clapping of a few hands when his dad was ousted from the congregation, taking his family with him.

That had been a long time ago, almost twenty years. He shrugged it off, the way he'd been trying to shrug it off since the day it happened. He walked down the hall and met his brother at the back door, coming in through the utility room. It had rained during the night and Wyatt's boots were muddy. He leaned against the dryer to kick them off.

Ryder reached for three-year-old Molly but she held tight to Wyatt. It was Kat, a year younger, who held her arms out, smiling the way little girls should smile. With one less child, Wyatt could hold the door and kick off his boots.

They would never know their mom. They wouldn't even remember her. But then, even in her life, Wendy hadn't been there for the girls. She had changed after having them. She had lost something and before any of them had figured it out, it had been too late to get her back.

"Long trip?" Ryder settled Kat on his hip and walked into the kitchen. The two-year-old smiled because his cheek brushed hers and he imagined it was rough.

"The longest." A year. That's what Ryder figured. His brother had been on a journey that had taken the last year of his life, and brought him back to Dawson.

"You girls hungry?"

"We ate an hour ago, just outside of Tulsa," Wyatt said. "I think they're probably ready to get down and play for a while. Maybe take a nap."

Ryder glanced at the little girl holding tight to his neck as he filled the coffeepot with water. "You want down, Chick?"

She shook her head and giggled.

"Want cookies?" he asked. When she nodded, he glanced at Molly. "You want cookies?"

She shook her head. She had big eyes that looked like the faucet was about to get turned on. She'd be okay, though. Kids had a way of bouncing back. Or at least that's what he thought. He didn't have a lot of experience.

"They don't need cookies this early," Wyatt interjected.

Older, wiser, Wyatt. Ryder shook his head, because he'd never wanted to grow up like Wyatt. He'd never wanted to be that mature.

"Well, I don't have much else around here." Ryder looked in the fridge. "Spoiled milk and pudding. I think the lunch meat went bad two days ago. It didn't taste real good on that last sandwich."

"Did it make you sick?" Molly whispered, arms still around Wyatt's neck in what looked like a death grip. He hadn't been around a lot of kids, but she was the timid kind. That was fine, he was a little afraid of her, too.

He'd had enough experience to know that kids could be loud and destroy much if left to their own devices.

"Nah, I don't get sick." He bounced Kat a little and she laughed.

"I guess I'll have to go to the store." Wyatt sat down at the dining room table.

"No, I'll get ready and go." Anything to get out of the house, away from this. He flipped on the dining room light. "Make a list and I'll drive into Grove. When I get home, we can run down to the Mad Cow before the church crowd gets there."

"I need to have the girls back in church. They like going."

"Yeah, kids do." They liked the crafts, the stories. He got that. He had liked it, too. "I need to feed the horses and then I'll get cleaned up and run to the store."

He brushed a hand through his hair and for the first time, Wyatt smiled. "Yeah, you might want to get a haircut."

"Probably." He slid his feet into boots and finished buttoning his shirt. "I guess just help yourself to anything you can find. The coffee's ready."

A brother and two kids, living in his house. Now that just about beat all. It was really going to put a kink in his life.

But then, hadn't Andie already done that? No, not Andie, not really.

When he walked out the back door, his dog, Bear, was waiting for him.

"Bear, this is not our life." But it was. He could look around, at the ranch his dad had built. He could smell rain in the air and hear geese on a nearby pond.

It was his life. But something had shaken it all up, leaving it nearly unrecognizable. Like a snow globe, shaken by some unseen hand. He looked up, because it was Sunday and a good day for thinking about God, about faith. He didn't go to church, but that didn't mean he had forgotten faith.

So now he had questions. How did he do this? His brother was home—with two kids, no less. His best friend was now his one-night stand. He had more guilt rolling around in his stomach than a bottle of antacid could ever cure.

Did this have something to do with his crazy prayers before he got on the back of a bull a month or so earlier. Did the words *God help me* count as a prayer? Or maybe it was payback for the bad things he'd done in his life?

Whatever had happened, he had to fix it—because he didn't like having his life turned upside down. But first he had to go to town and get groceries, something to feed two little girls.

Church had ended ten minutes ago and Andie had seen Ryder's truck driving past on his way to the farm. But they'd been stalled by people wanting to talk with she and her grandmother. Caroline had managed to smile and hang at the periphery of the crowds.

"We need to check on Ryder and Wyatt." Etta started her old Caddy, smiling with a certain pride that Andie recognized. Her granny loved that car. She'd loved it for more than twenty years, refusing to part with it for something new.

What could be more dependable, Etta always said, than a car that she'd taken care of since the day she drove it off the lot?

Dependable wasn't a word Andie really wanted to dwell on, not at that moment. Not when her grandmother was talking about Ryder.

"I think Ryder and Wyatt are able to take care of themselves." After her mother climbed into the front seat beside Etta, Andie slid into the back and buckled her seat belt. Etta eased through the church parking lot.

It hadn't been such a bad first Sunday back in church. The members of Dawson Community Church were friends, neighbors and sometimes a distant relative. They all knew her. Most of them knew that she'd gone on strike from church when Ryder stopped going. Because they'd been best friends, and a girl had to do something when her best friend cried angry tears over what his father had done, and over a moment in church that changed their lives. A girl had to take a stand when her best friend threw rocks into the creek with a fury she couldn't understand because life had never been that cruel to her.

Her strike had been more imaginary than real. Most of the time Etta managed to drag her along. But Andie had let her feelings be known. At ten she'd been pretty outspoken.

"How long have you known Ryder and Wyatt?" Caroline asked, and Andie wanted to tell her that she should know that. A mother should know the answer to that question.

"Forever." Andie leaned back in the seat and looked out the window, remembering being a kid in this very car, this very backseat. Her dad had driven and Etta had sat in the passenger side. The car had been new then. She'd been more innocent.

She'd heard them whispering about what Ryder's dad had done. She'd been too young to really get it. When she got home from church that day she'd run down the road and Ryder had met her in the field.

"Forever?" Caroline asked, glancing back over her shoulder.

"We've known each other since Ryder was five, and I was three. That's when they moved to Dawson. I guess about the time you left."

Silence hung over the car, crackling with tension and recrimination. Okay, maybe she'd gone too far. Andie sighed. "I'm sorry."

Etta cleared her throat and turned the old radio on low. "We'll stop by the Mad Cow and get takeout chicken. Knowing Ryder, he doesn't have a thing in that house for Wyatt and the girls to eat."

"What happened to Wyatt's wife?" Caroline asked.

Stop asking questions. Andie closed her eyes and leaned back into the leather seat. She wouldn't answer. She wouldn't say something that would hurt. She was working on forgiving. God had to know that wasn't easy. Shouldn't God cut her a little slack?

Etta answered Caroline's question. "She committed suicide last year. Postpartum depression."

It still hurt. Andie hadn't really known Wendy,

but it hurt, because it was about Ryder, Wyatt and two little girls.

"I'm so sorry." Caroline glanced out the window. "It isn't easy to deal with depression."

Clues to who her mother was. In a sense, Andie thought these might also be clues to who she was. She waited, wanting her mother to say more. She didn't. Etta didn't push. Instead she turned the Caddy into the parking lot of the Mad Cow. And Ryder was already there. He was getting out of his truck and a little girl with dark hair was clinging to his neck. He looked like a guy wearing new boots. Not too comfortable in the shoes he'd been forced to wear.

He saw them and he stopped. Etta parked next to his truck.

As they got out, Wyatt came around the side of the truck. The older of the two girls was in his arms. She didn't smile the way the other child smiled.

"We didn't beat the church crowd." Ryder tossed the observation to Wyatt but he smiled as he said it.

"No, you didn't, but you can eat lunch with us." Etta slipped an arm around Wyatt, even as she addressed the response at Ryder. "And you'll behave yourself, Ryder Johnson."

"I always do." He winked at the little girl in his arms and she giggled. And she wasn't even old enough to know what that wink could do to a girl, how it could make her feel like her toes were melting in her high heels.

Andie wished she didn't know what that wink could do to a girl. Or a woman. She didn't want to care that he looked cuter than ever with a two-year-old in his arms. He looked like someone who should have kids.

But he didn't want kids. He had never wanted children of his own. He said the only thing his childhood had prepared him for was being single and no one to mess up but himself.

"You look nice." He stepped closer, switching his niece to the opposite arm as he leaned close to Andie. "You smell good, too."

Andie smiled, because every answer seemed wrong. Sarcasm, anger, the words "Is this the first time you've noticed how I look?" and so on.

She didn't feel like fighting with him. She felt like going home to a cup of ginger tea and a good romance novel. She felt like hitching the trailer back to her truck and hitting the road with Dusty, because she could always count on her horse and the next rodeo to cheer her up. She could head down to Texas.

"You look a little pale." Caroline stood next to her, another problem that Andie didn't want to deal with. She felt like a tiny ant and people were shoveling stuff over the top of her, without caring that she was getting buried beneath it all.

"I'm fine."

"You really don't look so hot," Ryder added.

"You just said I look nice. Which is it, Ryder?"

"Nice, in a pale, illusive, gonna-kick-some-body-to-the-curb sort of way." He teased in the way that normally worked on her bad moods. Ryder knew how to drag her out of the pits.

But not today.

Today she wanted to be alone, to figure out the next phase of her life. And she didn't want to think about how Ryder would have to be a part of that future.

Or how he was going to feel about it.

Chapter Three

"**W**hy aren't you eating?" Ryder had tried to ignore Andie, the same way she'd obviously been ignoring him. She had talked to Wyatt, to the girls, even to her mother.

She was ignoring him the same way she was ignoring the chicken-fried steak on her dinner plate. And her mother was right. She did look pale.

"I'm eating." She smiled and cut a bite of the gravy-covered steak. "See."

She ate the bite, swallowing in a way that looked painful.

"Are you sick?"

She looked up to the heavens and shook her head. "No, I'm not sick."

"You act sick." He grinned a little, because he just knew he had to say what was on his mind. He couldn't stop himself. "You look like something the cat yacked up."

His nieces laughed. Even Molly. At least they appreciated his humor. He sat back in his chair, his hands behind his head, smiling at Andie. Kat giggled like she knew exactly what her Uncle Ryder had said. He hadn't expected to really like a two-year-old this much, but she already had him wrapped around her little finger.

He didn't think Andie was as thrilled with him. As a matter of fact she glared at him as if he was about her least favorite person on the planet. And with her mother, Caroline, sitting at the same table, he was pretty shocked that he'd be Andie's least favorite person.

"That's pleasant, Ryder. I'm sick of you asking me what's wrong. You haven't seen me in two months. Do you have something else you'd like to say to me?"

"Right here, right now?" That made his hands a little sweaty, especially when everyone at the table stared, including his nieces. Kat, who sat closest to him, looked a little worried. "No, I guess not. Well, other than wanting to know if you'd like to go the arena with me tonight. I could use a flank man."

"I'm not a man."

"Good point," Wyatt mumbled.

Ryder shot his brother a look. "Keep out of this."

Kat, two and innocent, clapped her hands and laughed.

A chair scooted on the linoleum floor. Ryder flicked his attention back to Andie. She was standing up, looking a little green and wobbly. Maybe it was the dress, or the three-inch heels. He stood, thinking he might have to catch her.

"What's wrong?" Etta started to stand up.

"I'm going outside. I need fresh air."

"I'll go with you." Ryder grabbed his hat off the back of the chair and moved fast, because she was practically running for the door.

She didn't go far, just to the edge of the building. He stood behind her as she leaned, gasping deep breaths of air.

"What's going on with you?"

"Stop." She kept her face turned, resting her forehead against the old concrete block building. "I must have caught something from Joy's kids when I stopped in Kansas. One of them was sick."

"I could take you home," he offered quietly, because he had a feeling she didn't need more questions at the moment.

"I'm fine now. I would just hate to make the girls sick. They don't need that." She turned, smiling, but perspiration beaded along her forehead and under her eyes. She was still pale.

"No," he agreed, "the girls don't need to get sick. I don't think I could handle that."

"They're just little girls."

"Yeah, and I'm not anyone's dad. That's Wyatt's job. He's always been more cut out for the husband and father gig."

And saying the words made him feel hollow on the inside, because he remembered standing next to Wyatt at his wife's funeral. He remembered what it felt like to stand next to a man whose heart was breaking.

Ryder hadn't ever experienced heartbreak and he didn't plan on it. He enjoyed his single life, without strings, attachments or complications.

"You're good with the girls," Andie insisted, his friend again, for the moment. "Just don't slip into your old ways, not while they're living with you."

"Right." He slid his hand down her back. "I'll be good. So, are you okay?"

"I'm good. I'm going back inside." She took a step past him, but he caught her hand and held her next to him.

"Andie, I don't want to lose my best friend. I'm sorry for that night. I'm sorry that I didn't walk away...before. And I'm sorry I walked away afterward."

She didn't look at him. He looked down, at the ground she was staring at—at dandelions peeking up through the gravel and a few pieces of broken glass. He touched her cheek and ran his finger down to her chin, lifting her face so she had to look at him.

"I'm sorry, too," she whispered. "I just don't know how to go back. We've always kept the line between us, Ryder. This is why."

"We don't have to stop being friends," he insisted, hoping he didn't sound like a kid.

"No, we don't. But you have to accept that things have changed."

"Okay, things have changed." More than things. She had changed. He could see it in her eyes in the way she smiled as she turned and walked away, back into the Mad Cow.

A crazy thought, that he had changed, too. He brushed it off and followed her into the diner. He hadn't changed at all. He still wanted the same things he'd always wanted. Some things weren't meant to be domesticated, like raccoons, foxes… and him.

When they got home, Andie changed into jeans and a T-shirt and headed for the barn. She was brushing Babe, her old mare, when Etta walked through the double doors at the end of the building.

"What's going on with you?" Etta, arm's crossed, stood with the sun to her back, her face in shadows.

The barn cat wandered in and Etta stepped away from the feline.

"There's nothing wrong." Andie brushed the horse's rump and the bay mare twitched her dark tail and stomped a fly away from her leg. "Okay, something is wrong. Caroline is here. I don't know what she wants from me. I don't know why she expects to walk into my life and have me happy to be graced with her presence."

"She doesn't expect that."

Andie stopped brushing and turned. "So now you're on her side."

"Don't sound like a five-year-old. I'm not on her side. I'm on your side. I want you to forgive her. I want you to have her in your life. I have to forgive her, too. She broke my son's heart. She broke your heart."

Andie shook off the anger. Her heart hadn't been broken, not by Caroline or anyone else.

"I'm fine." She brushed Babe's neck and the mare leaned toward her, her eyes closing slightly.

"You're not fine. And this isn't about Caroline, it's about you and Ryder. What happened?"

"Nothing. Or at least nothing a little time won't take care of."

Etta walked closer. "I guess it's too late for the talk that we should have had fifteen years ago," she said with a sigh.

Andie swallowed and nodded. And the words freed the tears that had been hovering. "Too late."

"It's okay." Etta stepped closer, her arm going around Andie's waist.

"No, it isn't. I messed up. I really messed up. This is something I can't take back."

"So you went to church?"

"Not just because of this. I went because I had to go. As much as I've always claimed I was strong, every time I was at the end of my rope, it was God that I turned to. I've always prayed. And that Sunday morning, I wanted to be in church."

"Andie, did you use…"

Andie's face flamed and she shook her head.

"Do you think you might be…"

They were playing fill-in-the-blank. Andie wanted option C, not A. She wanted the answer to be sick with a stomach virus. They didn't want to say the hard words, or face the difficult answers. She wasn't a fifteen-year-old kid. Funny, but until now she had controlled herself. She hadn't made these choices. She hadn't gotten herself into a situation like this.

She was trying to connect it all: her mistake,

her relationship with God, and her friendship with Ryder. How could she put it all together and make it okay?

"Maybe it's a virus. Joy's kids had a stomach virus."

"It could be." Etta patted her back. "It really could be."

And then a truck turned into the drive. Ryder's truck. And he was pulling a trailer. Andie closed her eyes and Etta hugged her close.

"You're going to have to tell him."

"I don't know anything, not yet. I don't know if I can face this. I'm trying so hard to get my act together and I can't pull Ryder into this."

"Soon." Etta kissed her cheek.

"When I know for sure."

Ryder was out of his truck. And he was dressed for roping, in his faded jeans, a black T-shirt and nearly worn-out roper boots.

"You going with me?" He tossed the question before he reached the barn. His grin was big, and he was acting as if there was nothing wrong between them. Andie wished she could do the same.

"I don't know."

Etta's brows went up and she shrugged. "I'm going in the house. I have a roast on and it needs potatoes."

Andie watched her grandmother walk away

and then she turned her attention back to Ryder. He scratched his chin and waited. And she didn't know what he wanted to hear.

"Come on, Andie, we've always roped on Sunday evenings."

It was what they'd done, as best friends. And they hadn't minded separating from time to time. She'd go out with James or one of the other guys. She'd watch, without jealousy, when he helped Vicki Summers into his truck. No jealousy at all.

Because they'd been best friends.

But today nausea rolled in her stomach and she couldn't think about leaving with him, or him leaving with Vicki afterward. And that wasn't the way it was supposed to happen.

"I can't go, not tonight."

"I don't want to lose you." He took off his white cowboy hat and held it at his side. "I wish we could go back and..."

"Think a little more clearly? Take time to breathe deep and walk away?" She shook her head. "We can't. We made a choice and now we have the consequences of that choice."

"Consequences? What consequences? You're the one acting like we can't even talk. It's simple. Just get in the truck and go with me."

"I can't." She tossed the brush into a bucket and the clang of wood hitting metal made Babe jump to the side. Andie whispered to the mare and reached to untie the lead rope from the hook on the wall. "I can't go with you, Ryder. I'm sick. My mom is here. I'm going to go inside and spend time with Etta."

"Fine." He walked to the door. "I'm going to be pretty busy in the next few weeks. Wyatt and the girls are going to need me."

"I know." She watched him walk away, but it wasn't easy. She'd never wanted to run after a guy the way she wanted to run after him, to tell him they could forget. They could go back to being friends, to being comfortable around each other. But she couldn't go after him and they couldn't go back.

She stood at the gate and watched as he climbed into his truck and slammed the door.

Ryder jumped into his truck and shifted hard into first gear. He started to stomp on it, and then remembered his horse in the trailer. Man, it would have felt good to let gravel fly. If only he could be sixteen again, not dealing with losing his best friend to a one-night mistake.

Why couldn't she just get over it and go with him? This was what they did, they went roping together. They hunted together. They got over things together.

As he eased onto the road he let his mind drift

back, to the night in Phoenix. Stupid. Stupid. Stupid. They'd both been hurting. He'd been upset by Wyatt's situation. She'd been hurting because her twin sister had arrived in town, bringing back the pain of being a kid rejected by her mother.

And then his thoughts made a big U-turn, shifting his memory back to the Mad Cow and Andie's pale face.

He was an idiot. An absolute idiot.

Consequences. He caught himself in time to keep from slamming on the brakes. He eased to the side of the road and stopped the truck. He sat there for a long minute thinking back, thinking ahead. Thinking this really couldn't be happening to him.

He leaned back in his seat and thought about it, and thought about his next move. A truck drove past and honked. He raised a hand in a half wave.

Glancing over his shoulder he checked the road in both directions and backed the trailer up, this time heading the way he'd come from, to Etta's and to Andie.

As he turned into the driveway, she was coming out of the barn. She stopped in the doorway, light against the dark interior of the barn, her blond hair blowing a little in the wind. She sighed, he could see her shoulders rise and fall and then she walked toward him. And he wondered what she would say.

He parked and got out of the truck, waiting because he didn't know what questions to ask or how to face the consequences of that night. It would have been easier to keep running. But this would have caught up with him eventually. It wasn't as if he could run from it.

When she reached him, they stared at each other. The wind was blowing a little harder and clouds, low and heavy with rain, covered the sun. Shadows drifted across the brown, autumn grass.

"You're back a little quicker than I expected." She smiled, and for a minute he thought it might have been his imagination, her pale skin, the nausea.

He rubbed his face and tried to think of how a man asked a woman, a friend, this question.

"I came back because I have to ask you something."

"Go ahead." She slipped her hands into her front pockets.

His gaze slipped to her belly and he didn't even mean for that to happen. It was flat, perfectly flat. She cleared her throat. He glanced up and her eyebrows shot up.

"I have a question." Man, he felt like a fifteen-year-old kid. "Are you, um, are you having a baby?"

Chapter Four

The question she hadn't even wanted to ask herself. Ryder, her best friend for as long as she could remember, was peering down at her with toffee-brown eyes that had never been more serious. He wasn't a boy anymore. She wasn't a kid.

And she didn't want to answer this question, not today. She didn't want to stand in front of him, with her heart pounding and her stomach still rolling a little. She looked away, to the field across the road. It was nothing spectacular, just a field with a few too many weeds and a few cattle grazing, but it gave her something else to focus on.

"Andie, come on, we have to talk about *this*."

"Like we talked two months ago? Come on, Ryder, admit that neither one of us want to talk about this."

He took off his hat and brushed his arm across

his forehead. He glanced down at her and shook his head. "No, maybe this isn't how I wanted to spend a Sunday afternoon, but this is what we've got."

"I don't want to talk about it. Not today."

"So you are...?"

"I don't know." She looked down, at dusty, hard-packed earth. At his boots and hers as they stood toe-to-toe in that moment that changed both of their lives. He was just a cowboy, the kind of guy who had said he'd never get married.

And she'd claimed his conviction as her own. Because that's what they had done for years. She had never been one of those girls dreaming of weddings, the perfect husband or babies. She didn't play the games in school with boys' names and honeymoon locations. Instead she'd thought about how to train the best barrel horse and what it would take to win world titles.

Babies. As much as she had wanted to pretend otherwise, her feminine side had caused her to go soft when she held a baby or watched children play. When she watched her friends with their husbands, she felt a little empty on the inside, because she shared her life with Etta—and with Ryder—but Ryder never shared his heart, not the way a woman wanted a man to share his heart.

"Andie, I'm sorry, this shouldn't have happened." He touched her cheek and then his hand dropped to his side and he stepped back a few steps.

"I definitely don't want you to be sorry." She looked up, trying her best to be determined. "Like I said, I don't know. It could be that I caught the stomach virus some of the kids in Kansas had. When I know for sure, I'll let you know."

"Let me know?" He brushed a hand through his hair and shoved his hat back in place, a gesture she'd seen a few too many times and she knew exactly what it meant. Frustration.

Well she could tell him a few things about frustration. But she wasn't in the mood. She wasn't in the mood to spell out for him that this hadn't been in her plans, either. He hadn't been in her plans, not this way.

"Yeah, I'll let you know. Look, whatever happens, whatever this is, it isn't going to change anything." She was glad she sounded firm, sounded strong. She felt anything but, with her insides quivering. "You've always been my friend and that's how it'll stay."

"What does that mean?"

"It means I'm not going to tie you down or try to drag you into this. It doesn't change things."

"I have news for you, Andie Forester, this changes things. This changes everything."

"It doesn't have to."

He shook his head. "Are you being difficult

for a reason, other than to just drive me crazy? If you're pre…uh, having a baby, it changes a lot, now doesn't it?"

She wanted to smile, because even the word brought a bead of sweat across his brow and his neck turned red. But she couldn't smile, not yet.

"I'll let you know when I find out for sure."

"Fine, you let me know. And we'll pretend that this isn't important, if that's what you really want." He turned and walked away, a cowboy in faded jeans, the legs worn and a little more faded where he'd spent a lot of time in the saddle.

He waved as he climbed into his truck and started the engine. She waved back. And it already felt different. She'd been lying to herself, trying to tell herself it wouldn't matter.

She watched him drive away and then she considered her next move. Go inside and face her mother, or stay in the barn and hide from reality. She liked the hiding plan the best. Facing Ryder and her mother, both in the same day, sounded like too much.

In the dark, dusty interior of the barn she could close her eyes and pretend she was the person she'd been two months ago. But she wasn't.

A lot had happened. She turned over a bucket and sat down. She leaned against the stall door behind her and closed her eyes. Everything had changed. Most importantly, she had changed.

On a Sunday morning in a church service at the rodeo arena she had changed. It had started when she walked out of her horse trailer, a cup of coffee in hand, and she'd heard the couple who led the service singing "Amazing Grace." She'd walked to the arena and taken a seat on a row of bleachers a good distance from the crowd.

During that service, God had pulled her back to Him. She had been drawn back into a relationship that she'd ignored for years. And it hadn't been God's fault that she'd walked away. It had been about her loyalty to Ryder.

She opened her eyes and looked outside, at a sky growing darker as the sun set. The days were cool and growing shorter. She wasn't ready for winter. She definitely didn't know how to face spring, and seven months from now.

How did a person go from turning back to God, to making a giant mistake like the one she'd made with Ryder? And what about God? Was He going to reject her now?

She'd had experience with rejection.

It had started with her mother. She squeezed her eyes shut again, and refused the tears that burned, tightening in her throat because she wasn't going to let them fall.

"Forgive me," she whispered, wanting peace,

something that settled the ache in her heart and took away the heaviness of misgivings.

She stood and walked into the feed room to look at the calendar tacked to the wall. It recorded dates and locations of rodeos. She thumbed back to the month of the Phoenix rodeo and tried to remember. She leaned, resting her forehead against the rough barn wood.

For two months she'd told herself there wouldn't be consequences, other than a little bit of time when they'd be uncomfortable with each other.

But she'd been wrong. There were definitely consequences, and this wasn't going away any time soon. She picked up the pencil she used to mark the calendar and she went through the next few months, marking through events she'd planned to attend, but now wouldn't.

Things had definitely changed.

Roping hadn't taken Ryder's mind off Andie and the possibility of a baby. His baby. He didn't need proof of that fact because he knew Andie. As he drove through Dawson after loading his horse and talking for a few minutes with friends, his mind kept going back, to better choices he could have made. And forward, to how his life would never be the same.

Ryder drove through Dawson. It was Sunday night and that meant there wasn't a thing going on and nothing open but the convenience store. A few trucks were parked at the side of the building and a few teenagers sat on tailgates, drinking sodas and eating corn dogs. Big night out in Dawson.

He turned left on the road that led out of town, to his family farm, and on past, to the house where Andie had grown up with Etta. He considered driving there and talking to her, trying to figure out what they were going to do. He didn't figure she'd be ready to talk.

Instead he pulled into his drive and drove back to the barn. As he got out, he noticed Wyatt in the backyard with the girls. Wyatt was sitting at the patio table, the girls were running around the yard with flashlights. They were barely more than babies.

And Wyatt didn't know what to do with them. That thought kind of sunk into the pit of his stomach. Wyatt had always been the one who seemed to know how to do this adult thing.

Ryder stepped out of the truck and walked back to the trailer to unload his horse. The big gelding stomped restlessly, ready to be out and ready to graze in the pasture.

"Easy up there, Buddy." Ryder unlatched the back of the trailer. He stepped inside, easing down the unused half of the trailer to untie the animal and back him out.

When they landed on firm ground, Wyatt was there. Ryder smiled at his brother and got a half smile in return. The girls had stopped running and were watching. They weren't used to horses. Wyatt had taken a job as a youth minister in Florida and they had lived in town.

"Long night?" Wyatt stepped back, watching.

"Yeah, kind of." How did he tell his brother? Wyatt had always held it together. He'd held them together as best he could.

"What's up?" Wyatt followed him to the gate, opening it for Ryder to let the horse out into the pasture.

"Nothing."

"Right."

Ryder pushed the gate closed and latched it. The horse reached for a bite of grass, managing to act like he hadn't eaten in days, not hours. Horses were easy to take care of. They could be left alone. They didn't make requirements. They had to be trained, but he was pretty sure they were a lot easier to train than a child.

He ranched. He raised quarter horses and black angus cattle. He didn't raise babies.

Until now.

The girls ran up to them, tiny things, not even reaching his hip. He closed the gate and turned his attention to Molly and Kat. And boots. They were wearing his boots. The good ones that had cost a small fortune.

He glanced up, pretty sure that God was testing him. This was a lesson on parenting, or patience. He didn't know which. Probably both.

"We like your shoes." Molly grinned, and he was happy to see her smiling. But man, she was wearing his best boots.

The look he gave Wyatt was ignored.

"Boots." Kat giggled. The pair she was wearing covered her legs completely.

"Yep, boots." He scooped up Kat and snuggled her close. She giggled and leaned back. She looked a lot like her mom. That had to be hard for Wyatt. Kat had Wendy's smile, her dimples, her laughter.

And she was a dirty mess. Mud caked her, and his boots. From the tangles in her hair, he guessed it had been a couple of days since it had seen a brush.

"You need a bath." He held her tight as they headed toward the house.

Kids needed things like baths, and their teeth brushed. They had to be tucked in and someone had to be there for them. They didn't need parents who drank themselves into a stupor and made choices that robbed a family of security.

He didn't drink. He had one thing going for him.

Anger knocked around inside him. The past had a way of doing that, and a guy shouldn't get angry thinking of parents who had died too young.

"If you need to talk…" Wyatt followed him up the steps to the back door, and then he shrugged. They'd never been touchy-feely. Sharing was for afternoon talk shows, not the Johnson brothers. They'd always solved their problems, even dealt with their anger, by roping a few calves or riding hard through the back field.

Every now and then they'd had a knock-down-drag-out in the backyard. Those fights had ended with the two of them on their backs, staring up at the sky, out of breath, but out of anger.

Talking about it didn't seem like an option.

"Yeah, I know we can talk." Ryder put his niece down on the floor and flipped on the kitchen light. Kat stomped around in his boots, leaving dirt smudges on the floor he'd mopped last night. "Did you guys eat?"

He looked around. There was an open loaf of bread on the counter and a jar of peanut butter, the lid next to it. He glanced down at Kat. She had a smear of peanut butter on her cheek. He twisted the bread closed.

"Did you feed the girls?" Ryder asked again when Wyatt hadn't answered.

"Molly made sandwiches."

"And you think that's good?" A three-year-old making sandwiches. Ryder screwed the lid on the peanut butter because he had to do something to keep from pushing his brother into a wall to knock sense into him. "Girls, are you hungry?"

Kat grinned and Molly looked at her dad. Ryder exhaled a lot of anger. He didn't have a clue what little kids ate. Wyatt should have a clue. If Wyatt couldn't do this, how in the world was Ryder going to manage?

"Tell you what, I'll make eggs and toast. Do you like eggs?" Ryder opened the fridge door.

"I can do it." Wyatt took the carton of eggs from his hands.

"You girls go play." Ryder smiled at his nieces. "I think there's a box of toys in the living room. Mostly horses and cowboys."

His and Wyatt's toys that Ryder had dug out of a back closet the night before.

When the girls were gone, he turned back to his brother. Wyatt cracked eggs into a bowl and he didn't look up. "I've taken care of them for a year."

"Yeah, I know you have."

The dog scratched at the back door. Ryder pushed it open and let the animal in, because there was one thing Bear was good at, and that was cleaning up stuff that dropped on the floor. Stuff like peanut butter sandwiches.

Bear sniffed his way into the kitchen and licked the floor clean, except he left the mud. Not that Ryder blamed him for that.

The dog was the best floor sweeper in the country.

"I'm taking care of my girls." Wyatt poured eggs into the pan. "And I don't want tips from a guy who hasn't had kids, or hasn't had a relationship in his life that lasted more than a month."

"That's about to change." Ryder muttered and he sure hadn't meant to open that can of worms. He'd meant to butter toast.

"What's that mean?" Wyatt turned the stove off.

"Remember what it was like, growing up in this house?"

"Sure, I remember." Wyatt scooped eggs onto four plates. "Always laughter, mostly the drunken kind that ended in a big fight by the end of the night. And then there were the phone calls."

Phone calls their mother received from the other women. Ryder shook his head, because memories were hard to shake. His dad's temper had been hard to hide from.

"Right. That's not the kind of life our kids should have." Ryder let out a sigh, because he had been holding on to those memories for a long time.

"Well, as far as I know, the only kids in this

house are mine, and they're not going to have that life, not in this house. If you're insinuating…"

"I'm not insinuating anything about you or how you're raising those girls." Ryder tossed a slice of buttered toast to his blue heeler. "Wyatt, there isn't a person around who blames you for having a hard time right now."

"I guess this isn't about me, is it?"

No, but it would have been nice to pretend it was. Ryder shrugged and poured himself a cup of that morning's coffee. He ignored his brother and slid the coffee into the microwave.

"No, it isn't about you." He took his cup of day old coffee out of the microwave. "I'm going outside."

Because it was still his life. For now.

"Not again." Andie rolled out of bed and ran for the bathroom. She leaned, eyes closed and taking deep breaths until the moment passed. When it was just a rolling hint of nausea, she sat back, leaning against the cool tile walls of her bathroom.

"I have gingersnaps."

She turned and Etta was standing in the doorway, already dressed for her day. Andie looked down at her own wrinkled pajamas that she honestly didn't want to change out of, not today.

"I'm not sure what good cookies and milk will do now."

Etta laughed. "Ginger for nausea. Although the milk might not be the best thing right now. Maybe ginger tea. Come downstairs and we'll see what I have."

The thought of ginger in tea made it worse. Andie closed the bathroom door with her foot and resumed position next to the commode. Her grandmother knocked, insistent. It wasn't a good thing, Etta's insistence, not this morning.

"Give me a minute, Gran."

"It's your mother."

Oh, that didn't make it better. Mother. Andie leaned again, perspiration beaded her brow and her skin felt clammy. She stood and leaned over the sink, turning on cold water to splash her face.

"Leave me alone."

"I can't. Etta said you're sick. Can I help?"

"No, you can't help." No one could help.

But there was a clear feeling that someone could. She closed her eyes and prayed for answers, because she'd never needed answers more. She felt like she was on a traffic circle in the middle of a foreign city and she didn't know which road to take, so she kept driving around the circle, looking for the right direction, the right path.

Her own analogy and it made her dizzy. She opened her eyes and the swaying stopped.

"Andie?"

"I'm fine. I'll be out in a minute."

The door moved a little, like someone leaned against it from the other side. "I know you're angry with me."

The woman wouldn't give up.

And the term *angry with her mother* didn't begin to describe the hurt, rejection and fury, all rolled into one giant ball and lodged in her heart. Andie slid her hand over her stomach, wondering at the idea of a baby growing inside her, and wondering how a mother could leave a child behind.

People did things even they didn't understand, things they regretted. She tried not to think about Phoenix, but it wouldn't go away. Ryder's face, his smile swimming in her vision, couldn't be blinked away.

She had always cared about his rotten hide.

Hormones. All of this emotion was caused by raging hormones. She had to stop, to get her act together. She dried her face off and pulled the door open.

Her mother nearly fell on top of her.

"I forgive you." Andie walked past her mother and kept going, down the stairs, out the front door. Alyson's cat greeted her on the front porch. She scooped the kitten up and held it close. Not that she liked cats. But she had to do something.

The screen door creaked open.

"Are you pregnant?" Caroline asked as she stepped onto the porch. She looked so pinched and worried, Andie nearly smiled.

"I probably am." She glanced away from her mom. "I guess this is how you expected I'd end up."

"I never thought you'd be less than wonderful. I didn't take Alyson because I thought she'd be better." Caroline swept her hand over her face, her fingers glittering with gold and gems. "I took her because she was easier. You had so much energy. You pushed me."

"Pushed you?"

"I knew I couldn't be a good mother to you. I was worried I'd be a horrible mother. That would have been worse for you, wouldn't it?"

"You could have called."

"It seemed better this way. I can't go back, Andie. But I do want you to know that I'm here if you need me."

"I'm sure I'll be fine."

"Of course you'll be fine. If you'd like, I could go to the doctor with you before I leave in the morning."

The kitten hissed and clawed, wanting down. Andie let him go, watched him scamper with his scrawny tail in the air and then she turned to meet her mother's cautious gaze. "I get that you want to be forgiven, but we can't undo twenty-five years of silence with a doctor's appointment and you standing outside the bathroom door offering words of support."

"I know that." Caroline hugged herself, her arms thin. "Will you call if you need anything before I come back next month to help Alyson finish the wedding plans?"

"I'll call." Andie sighed. "If it helps, I don't hate you. I wanted to, but I don't."

Caroline nodded and tears flooded her eyes. "I'm glad."

"Yeah, so am I." Andie sat down on the steps, her mother stood, leaning against the post. "I guess what you have to realize is that I'm not ready for you to play the part of my mother."

"Right. Of course." Caroline nodded and stepped away from the post. "Thank you for giving me a chance."

"You're welcome." The kitten crawled into Andie's lap, twitching its tail in her face.

Andie watched her mother walk back into the house, and then a truck was barreling down the paved road and turning into their driveway. She groaned and wondered how a day could turn this bad this fast.

Instead of sitting on the porch, waiting for him

to get to her, she got up and walked inside. From the front hallway she could smell the spicy aroma of the ginger tea that Etta had promised. And now it seemed like a good idea.

Etta turned to look at her when she walked into the kitchen. Her grandmother pointed to the cup on the counter and Andie picked it up, holding it up to inhale the aroma of ginger and cinnamon.

"Sip it and see if that doesn't help settle your stomach."

Etta flipped pancakes onto a plate.

"If it does, I want a few of those pancakes." Andie sat down with the tea and watched her grandmother. It was just the two of them, the way it had been for a long time. Even when Andie's dad had been alive, it had been Etta and Andie most of the time.

"The first plate is yours." Etta glanced out the kitchen window. "You know that Ryder is here, right?"

"I know." She sipped the tea and waited, listening for the familiar sound of his steps on the porch, the song he whistled that wasn't a song and the mew of the kitten when she had someone cornered for attention.

Chapter Five

Ryder walked up the back steps to Etta's, whistling, pretending it was any other fall day in Oklahoma. It was easy to whistle. Not so easy to put out of his mind other thoughts, more complicated thoughts.

He rapped on the back door and Etta called out for him to come in, that he didn't have to knock. He'd never knocked before, but he thought that today might be a little different. Things had definitely changed.

Andie sat on a stool just inside the door. She turned to look at him, and then shifted her attention back to the cup in her hand, and the plate of pancakes in front of her. She looked a little pale, a little green. Her hair was in a short ponytail with thin wisps hanging loose to frame her face.

How many times had he seen her in the morning? They'd taken predawn rides together, worked cattle together and hauled hay together. But today she was maybe the mother of his child. Stuff shifted inside him, trying to make room for that idea. It wasn't easy to have that space when he'd never thought about his life in terms of fatherhood.

He felt nearly as sick as she must feel.

"You're up and around early." She kept her focus on the plate of pancakes.

"Yeah, well, I have a lot to do today."

"Like?"

"First of all, I want to talk to you."

"Talk away." She took another bite of pancake.

Okay, she wasn't going to make this easy. He leaned against the wall next to the door and watched her eat. He had just finished breakfast at the Mad Cow, but that didn't stop him from thinking about Etta's pancakes. No one made them like Etta.

"Want some?" Andie offered, smiling a little. Looking a little like her old self.

"Nah, I just ate. Andie, we need to talk."

"I'd rather not. I mean, really, what do you need to say? We've covered it. We made a mistake. We were both there. So we move on, we find a way to keep being friends."

"I think I should give you kids some privacy?" Etta turned off the stove and slipped the apron over her head, hanging it on the hook as she walked out the door.

"We don't need privacy." Andie stood, picking up her empty plate. She carried it to the sink and ran water over it, staring out the window.

Ryder walked up behind her, wanting to hold her. And that surprised him. She'd never been that person to him, the person he dated, the person he held. She'd been the person who helped him keep his act together, and the friend he turned to when he needed to talk something out. He'd been that person for her, too.

"We need privacy." He stepped next to her, leaning shoulder to shoulder for a second. And she leaned back, resting her head against him.

"Okay, we're alone." She glanced up, turning to face him.

Yeah, they were alone. He took a few deep breaths and told himself this was the right thing to do. Andie was staring up at him, blue eyes locking with his. His emotions tangled inside him like two barn cats were going at it, fighting to the death inside his stomach.

"I never thought I'd do this." He'd ridden two-thousand-pound bulls, fought fires with the volunteer fire department, and he'd never been this afraid of anything.

"Do what?"

He reached into his pocket and held out his hand. "Andie, I think we should get married."

And she laughed at him. He stepped back, not sure how to react to laughter. He had kind of expected her to be mad, or something. She could have cried. But he hadn't expected laughter.

"You've got to be kidding me."

"Well, no, I wasn't." But maybe he should pretend it had been a joke. They could laugh it off and move on like it hadn't happened. Maybe she'd even tell him this was a late April Fools' joke, and she wasn't going to have a baby.

"Well, you should be kidding. You know you don't want to marry me. You don't want to marry anyone, and especially not like this."

"I'd marry you. Seriously, who better to marry than your best friend?"

She didn't make a sarcastic remark or roll her eyes, and those would have been the typical Andie reactions to his comment. Instead she smiled and he couldn't believe two months of hormones could change a woman that much, that fast.

"I'm not going to marry you, Ryder. We won't even know for sure if I'm pregnant until I go to the doctor tomorrow."

"We could get a, well, one of those tests."

She turned a little pink and looked down at the floor. Her feet were bare and she wore sweats cut off at the knees and a T-shirt. She looked young.

And he felt older than dirt.

"Andie?"

"I took a test." She turned away from him, running dishwater like nothing was different, as if this was a normal day and he hadn't just had his proposal, his very first proposal, rejected. As if she hadn't just admitted to taking a pregnancy test.

He shoved his hands into his pockets and waited a few seconds before pushing further into the conversation.

"Okay, you took a test. I guess you didn't think I had a right to know?"

"Yes, I was going to let you know." She kept washing dishes without looking at him. "I took the test last night and it was positive."

So, this was how it felt to learn you were going to be a dad. Not that he hadn't already been pretty sure, but this made it official. She reached for the ring where he'd left it on the counter. It had been his grandmother's. She looked at it for a long moment and then she smiled and put it back in his hand.

"Save your ring for someone you love. I'm going to have this baby, and I'm not going to force you into its life, or my life. I'm not going to accept a proposal you probably planned while you were feeding cattle this morning."

She knew him that well.

"Now, if you don't mind, I have a lot to do today. Rob's coming over to shoe my horses and Caroline is going back to Boston tomorrow."

Andie was trying like crazy not to be hurt or mad. She'd never wanted a proposal like this, one that a guy felt as if he had to make. She hadn't spent too much of her life thinking about marriage, but she knew the one thing she wanted. She wanted love. She didn't want to start a marriage based on "have to."

That night two months ago was one she couldn't undo. She couldn't undo the consequences. She closed her eyes and her hand went to her stomach. As much as she had never thought about babies in connection with her life, she couldn't think of this baby as a punishment.

It was her baby. She opened her eyes and Ryder was watching her. It was his baby, too. Having a baby changed everything, for both of them. It changed who they were and who they were going to be. It changed their friendship.

If she had to do it over again, she would have walked away from Ryder that night in Phoenix. She would have stopped things. Because a baby's life shouldn't start like this, with parents who could barely look at one another.

A baby should be planned, shouldn't it? A baby should know that it was being born into a home with two parents prepared to love it and raise it.

So what did a person do when the perfect plan hadn't happened? Andie figured they made the best of things. They counted from this day forward and promised to do their best after this.

"When are you going to the doctor?"

"Tomorrow." She washed a plate and he took it from her to run under rinse water.

"I meant, what time?"

"I'm going to leave early, probably by nine."

"I'll take you."

Andie stopped washing and took a deep breath. "I don't need you to take me."

"Why in the world are you pushing me away?" Ryder's voice was low, calm. But she knew better. She knew him better. "If you're pregnant, I'm the father. Right?"

"Right."

"So, I'm going with you. My baby, Andie. That has to give me some rights. Maybe you don't want to marry me, but I don't think you'll stop me from being a part of this kid's life."

"I'm not trying to stop you. I'm trying to tell you that I'm not expecting this from you."

Her insides shook and she felt cold and clammy as a wave of nausea swept through her again. Ryder touched her arm, his hand warm on her bare skin.

"Do you need to sit down?"

"Yes, I need to sit down and I need for you to stop acting like this."

"How do you want me to act?"

"I don't know." She let him lead her to one of the bar stools at the kitchen counter.

"Well, that makes two of us, Andie. We're both in a place we never expected to be. We're going to be parents. That's going to take some time to adjust to. Give me a break and don't expect me to know exactly what to say or how to react."

"Fine, then you give me a break and don't expect me to suddenly think of you as my handsome prince." She blinked away tears. "You've always been my toad."

He smiled and shook his head and she thought he might hug her, but he didn't. As she was contemplating the dozens of reasons why she shouldn't want him to hug her, his cell phone rang.

Andie waited, watching as he talked, as his expression changed from aggravated with her to worried.

"I'll be right there." He slipped his cell phone

into his pocket. He met her gaze and his eyes were no longer dancing with laughter.

"What's up?"

"Molly's sick. Wyatt needs to run to town and get something for her. My medicine cabinet doesn't support the needs of toddlers."

"I can go with you." Andie hopped off the bar stool and grabbed her cell phone that had been charging all night. "Let me get shoes."

"You're sick."

"I'm fine. It's over now." She tried to smile, but he was still watching her. She was suddenly breakable.

He'd have to get over that in a real hurry.

"Morning sickness, Ryder. Morning, and then it goes away."

"Right. I get it."

The back door opened. Etta walked in, glancing from one to the other, clearly looking for marks of a fight.

"Where are you two off to?" Etta kicked off her shoes and set a basket of fresh eggs on the counter.

"Molly's sick," Andie explained as she leaned to tie her shoes. "I'm going over to see if there's anything I can do."

"You're going to help?" Etta smiled a little. "With children?"

"I can do that."

"Call if you need my help."

"Will do." Andie hugged her grandmother. "Oh, if Rob gets here before I get back, tell him Dusty and Babe need shoes. Not that he won't be able to tell."

"Of course."

Ryder pushed the door open and Andie walked out, past him, his arm brushing hers. And then he walked next to her. They didn't talk. When had they ever not talked? They'd always had something to say to one another, something to tease the other about.

How did she get that back? Or did she? Maybe that was the other consequence, losing her best friend.

Ryder opened the passenger side truck door. For her. She stopped and gave him a look. "Stop." She stood in front of him.

"Stop what?"

"When have you ever opened the car for me?"

"I don't know. I'm sure I've done it before. Would you just get in?"

She shrugged and climbed in. "Sure thing."

The door closed and he walked around the front of the truck to the driver's side. Her heart clenched a little, because he was sweet and gorgeous and a cowboy. For most of her life she'd just seen him as the friend she couldn't live without.

Now, watching him walk away, she wondered if she'd kept that line between them because he'd insisted on just being friends.

No, that wasn't it. She was just being overly emotional. She didn't love Ryder. He didn't love her. And maybe, just maybe, the test was wrong. She'd go to the doctor tomorrow and find out it had all been a big mistake. They'd laugh and go back to being who they had always been.

Ryder didn't talk to Andie on the short drive to his place. As he eased the truck up the driveway, he let his gaze settle on the house he'd grown up in. It was a big old ranch house that his parents had remodeled. They'd added the new windows, the brick siding and the landscaping.

It had sheltered them, but it hadn't exactly been a happy home. Wyatt and Ryder had spent their time breaking horses, roping steers and looking out for each other.

They'd been in more than their share of fights. They'd broken more than a few hearts. He knew that. He could accept that he'd always been the bad boy that most parents didn't want to see walk through the door to pick up their little girl for a date.

And now he was going to be a dad. The idea itched inside him, like something he was deathly allergic to. But when he walked through the front door and saw three-year-old Molly on the sofa, a stuffed animal in her arms and her little face red from the fever that must have come on since he left the house, he thought different things about being a dad.

He thought about a kid of his own, one that he wouldn't let down.

But what if he did? What if he messed up a kid the way his parents had messed him up? What if his kid grew up too independent for its own good, or always afraid of what was happening in the living room?

The last thing he should be thinking of was a little girl with Andie's eyes.

Wyatt held Kat. "Can you watch them while I run to Grove and get some medicine?" The little girl looked like she might be nearly asleep, but when she saw Ryder she smiled. And then she held her arms out to Andie.

And Andie's eyes widened. "Oh, okay."

She held the little girl and when she looked over Kat's shoulder at him, he felt like someone who didn't belong in this picture. Andie probably felt the same way.

"I'll be right back." Wyatt grabbed his keys, shot a look over his shoulder and walked out the front door.

Something about that look had Ryder worrying that his brother wouldn't come back. He walked to the door and watched the truck drive away. "How about some lunch?"

He turned, smiling at Kat, and then Molly. His dog, Bear, was curled on the couch at her feet. As Ryder approached her side, Bear looked up, letting out a low growl. So, it had been that easy to steal the dog's loyalty? It just took being a little girl with big eyes.

"Bear, enough." At the warning, the dog's stub tail thumped the leather sofa.

Molly's eyes watered. Ryder sat down on the coffee table, facing her. "How about a drink of water?"

She nodded and sat up, still dressed in her nightgown with a princess on the front. His heart filled up in a way he'd never experienced. And then it ducked for cover, because this couldn't be his life.

Movement behind him. He turned and Andie was sitting in the rocking chair, Kat held against her. If Wyatt was running, he should have taken Ryder with him.

"Is her forehead hot?" Andie asked, her voice soft, comforting. He'd never heard it like that, as if she already knew how to be a mom.

Maybe women were that way? Maybe they had that natural instinct, and only men had to wonder and worry that they'd never get it right. The way he was worrying.

He touched Molly's head. "Pretty hot." He winked at the little girl as she curled back into her blanket, his dog curling into the bend of her knees.

"Maybe get a cool, wet cloth?" Andie shrugged. "I really don't have a clue, but it could be a while before Wyatt gets back and maybe cool water would bring her temperature down. We could call Etta."

"Wyatt will come back." Ryder cleared his throat. "I mean, he'll be back soon. It doesn't take that long to drive into Grove."

"Right." She was still holding Kat, her fingers stroking the little girl's brown hair. "Do you have a brush? Her hair's kind of scraggly."

He stood up. "I'll get a wet cloth for Molly and a brush for Kat."

When he walked back into the room, Molly was dozing and Kat had found a book for Andie to read. The two of them were cuddled in his big chair, Andie's bare feet on the ottoman.

His throat tightened and he looked away, because it was a lot easier to deal with Molly and not the crazy thoughts going through his mind.

Wyatt came back.

Andie breathed a sigh of relief when he walked through the door an hour later. He had a bag of medication and two stuffed animals. He avoided looking at her, and at Ryder. She wondered if he had thought about not coming back.

How did a person go on when the person they had loved the most, the one they had promised to cherish and protect, took their own life? She couldn't imagine his emotions, the loss, the guilt and the questions.

The questions about her mother leaving didn't begin to compare to what Wyatt must be asking himself every single day. She wanted to tell him he couldn't have stopped it. She wanted to tell him that people make choices, and when they're making those choices they aren't always thinking about how the ones left behind will feel. Wendy wouldn't have wanted to hurt him, or her daughters.

It wasn't her place. She and Wyatt had never been close. He'd been older, wiser and never up for any of her and Ryder's crazy antics.

She shifted and he moved, as if he had just noticed her. Kat had fallen asleep in her arms and Molly was sleeping on the couch. Andie looked at Ryder. Without words, he took the sleeping child from her arms and placed her on the opposite end of the couch from her sister.

Bear hopped down, looking offended the way only a dog can.

"We should get you back before Rob gets there to shoe those horses." Ryder had walked to the door. His gaze settled first on the girls and then on Wyatt. "Need anything before we go?"

"No, we're fine. Thanks for watching them."

"No problem. Call if you need me."

As they walked out to the truck, Andie slowed her pace.

"Do you think he'll be okay?" She glanced back at the house. Ryder followed the direction of her gaze and shrugged.

"I guess he will. What else can he do?"

"I guess you're right. But I can't imagine…"

"Yeah, I know."

His hand reached for hers. Andie didn't say anything. She walked next to him, his fingers tightly laced through hers. When they got to the truck he squeezed lightly and then let go. His hand was on the door handle, but he didn't open it.

Andie reached to do it herself, but he stopped her.

"Andie, we're going to figure this out. I don't know how, but we will. I guess we'll do it the way we've always faced everything else—together."

She nodded, but her eyes were swimming and she just wanted him to hold her hand again. She didn't want to feel alone. His words had taken away a little of that feeling and replaced it with hope. Maybe they would survive this.

"We should go." Andie glanced away, but

Ryder touched her cheek, drawing her attention back to him, forcing her to meet his gaze. She stared up at him, at lean, suntanned cheeks and a smile that curved into something delicious and tempting.

That smile was her downfall. She should turn away and not think about her life in terms of being in Ryder's life. She should definitely look away. But his eyes were dark and pulled her in.

"We should definitely go," she repeated, whispering this time.

"I know, but there's one thing we need to do before we leave."

He leaned, his hand still on her cheek. Her fingers slipped off the chrome door handle to rest on his arm.

His lips touched hers in a gesture that was sweet and disarming. His hand moved from her cheek to the back of her neck and he paused in the kiss to rest his forehead against hers.

Andie gathered her senses, because she couldn't let her heart go there, not in the direction it wanted to go.

"We shouldn't have gone there." She broke the connection and reached for the door handle. This time he opened it for her.

"Andie, at least give me a chance to figure this all out before you give up on me."

"I've never given up on you." She touched his

arm. "But I can't be distracted, Ryder. I have to make the right decisions, now more than ever."

"And you think turning down my proposal was the right decision?"

"Yeah, right now it is. It was sweet of you, really it was, but it was spur-of-the-moment and this is something that we should take time to think about."

Spur-of-the-moment was definitely a bad idea.

Chapter Six

Andie walked through the glass doors of the women's health clinic the next morning and she couldn't deny that her stomach was doing crazy flips and her palms were sweating. This time it was a good old case of nerves and not morning sickness. She rubbed her hands down the sides of her jeans and ignored the cautious look Ryder shot her as they walked across the granite-tiled lobby.

"We could skip this. I mean, the test is probably right."

Ryder laughed a little as he pushed the button on the elevator. "Right, we already know, so why bother with a doctor? I mean, who needs help delivering a kid into the world?"

Every word spiked into her heart. *Delivering. Kid. World.* This baby wasn't going to stay inside her, where it was safe, where it was a thought, something in the future. It would come kicking and screaming into her life. If Etta's calculations were correct, it would happen in May. Spring.

Andie wouldn't be riding for a world title any time soon.

But with the life growing inside of her, that couldn't be her focus. Her old plans were being replaced by new ones. Etta was looking at paint samples and fabric for baby quilts.

It was a little soon for that.

They got off the elevator at the third floor. Andie stood in the wide corridor, staring at Suite 10. Another couple stepped off the second elevator, smiling, holding hands. The other woman's belly was round and her eyes were shining with anticipation. And Andie didn't know how to reach for Ryder's hand, or how to make this about a happy future for the two of them. The three of them.

Her own belly was still flat. Her jeans still fit. Other than nausea in the morning and a positive sign on a stick, this didn't seem real. But it was.

At least Ryder was with her. Of course he was. She knew him well enough to know that he wasn't going to let her go through this alone. He just wasn't going to be the person with adoration in his eyes, holding her hand and telling her he'd always be there for her.

He'd never been that person for anyone. She knew him, knew that he'd worked hard at never letting himself get too involved. He didn't even want kids.

That was one thought she wished she would have blocked. Too late, though, because it had obviously already been swimming around in her mind.

"We're going to be late." Ryder reached for the door and glanced back at her. "Andie, you coming with me? I'm pretty sure this doctor doesn't want to examine me."

She tried to smile. "I'm coming."

They stepped into a prenatal world of soft colors, relaxing music and mothers-to-be reading magazines as they waited. The bad case of nervousness she was already experiencing went into overdrive. It was bad enough to make her reach for Ryder's hand, tugging him close.

"Relax." He walked with her to the counter. The receptionist smiled up at him. He grinned with that wicked Ryder charm that had kept girls following him since kindergarten. "Andie Forester. We have an appointment."

"Right. Here's the paperwork for new patients, Mr. Forester." The young woman handed over a clipboard with a pen and a stack of papers to be filled out.

Ryder turned, handing Andie the clipboard. "There you go, Mrs. Forester."

She smacked him with the clipboard. "You're horrible."

He winked. "Yeah, I work at it. But you're color is coming back, so that's a plus."

She walked away from him and he followed. When she sat down in a corner, as far away from other patients as she could get, he sat down next to her. He crossed his right leg over his left knee and leaned back in the chair that had to be one of the most uncomfortable she'd ever sat in.

While she filled out paperwork, he flipped through magazines, giggling a little bit like a junior-high kid with the lingerie catalogue. She shot him a dirty look and he didn't even manage to look contrite.

Thirty minutes later, Andie walked through the doors of the exam room, alone. Other women had taken their husbands, the father's of their babies. Ryder wasn't her husband. And she couldn't face this with him.

She didn't know how to face it without him. She sat down on the examining table and waited for the doctor. And she waited. She glanced at her watch and groaned, it was way past noon. No wonder she was getting shaky. Baby needed to eat. An OB should know that.

The door opened. Andie's hands were shaking.

She twirled them in the robe she'd been told to wear by the nurse who had made a brief stop some thirty minutes earlier.

"Sorry, had an emergency." Dr. Mark looked down at his file. "Good news. You're pregnant."

He said it with a happy smile that faded when he looked at her face.

"That is good news, isn't it?" he asked, pushing his glasses to the top of his head. His hair was blond and thinning, his smile was kind and fatherly. She liked him.

"It is." She bit down on her lip, trying to stop the trembling. "I'm sorry. It's not really a surprise. You can't be sick for days on end and really be shocked by the news that you're pregnant."

"But it isn't something you planned. I'm assuming it is something you plan to keep?"

Heat rushed to her cheeks. She'd never thought of anything other than keeping this baby. Her baby. She blinked a few times.

"Of course I'm keeping my baby."

"Of course." He smiled and sat down. "I'm going to do a quick exam, but first we'll do an ultrasound. If the father is here, he can come back…"

"No, he can't. I mean. This isn't what either of us planned. We're not, we're not in a relationship."

It sounded pathetic. Not in a relationship, but having a baby. She buried her face in her hands and waited for her cheeks to cool to their normal temperature.

"This doesn't have to be the end of the world." Dr. Mark patted her arm. "It's a different path than you probably had planned for yourself. It's going to take some adjusting, to make this work out. But I think you can do it."

Andie looked up, meeting eyes that were kind, with crinkled lines of age and experience at the corners.

"Yeah, I know I can make it."

She wanted to ask him what he thought about God. She had developed a new relationship with God, and then she'd realized she was pregnant. Some people might think the baby pushed her back into church. But it had been her own feelings, her own desire to have that connection that had taken her to that service.

The baby hadn't pushed her there.

"Andie, if you need someone to talk to..."

She shook her head. "I'm fine, really. It's just a lot to adjust to."

She put on a big smile, to prove to him, and maybe to herself, that she was okay.

"Okay then, let's go for that ultrasound. Down the hall, second door on the left. I'll be right there. And we'll take a picture for dad. We don't want him to miss out on everything."

Right. She nodded and hopped down from the table.

"What about activity. I mean, horseback riding? Work?"

"Within reason you can continue activities that you've been doing on a regular basis. Of course you don't want to do anything strenuous, or dangerous."

"Got it." She walked out, down the hall to the room he'd directed her to. Alone.

She was going to see her baby, or what would soon be her baby, and she wished someone was there with her. She wished Etta had come with her. She wished Ryder had insisted. If he had pushed... She shook off that thought, because she shouldn't make him push.

Instead of having someone with her, she walked into a darkened room alone and a nurse helped her onto the bed.

A few minutes later she raised her head and watched the screen, saw the beating heart of her baby and she cried. Dr. Mark handed her a tissue.

"A healthy heart." He removed the ultrasound and the nurse wiped her belly. "Here's your baby's first picture."

Andie took the black-and-white photo, her

fingers trembling as she held it up and looked at something that really looked like nothing. Except for that beating heart. Proof that her baby was alive. She couldn't wait to show Etta, and to call Alyson. She didn't want to think about Ryder. Not yet.

"Now remember what I said—make an appointment for one month from today with my colleague near Grove, Dr. Ashford. That'll be a lot easier than driving to Tulsa." Dr. Mark opened the door for her. "And try not to worry. Things have a way of working out for the best."

She nodded and tried not to attach his words of wisdom to the verse that all things work together for good. For those who trust. She had to trust. She had to believe that God would take what she had done on a night when she hadn't been thinking about Him, or trusting Him, and He would work it out for her good.

But one question kept running through her mind. Why should He?

When she walked into the waiting room, Ryder was there. He wasn't relaxed. He wasn't reading a book. He was pacing. She smiled and watched, because he hadn't seen her yet.

He had dressed up for the occasion, wearing jeans that weren't so faded and boots that weren't scuffed. He'd gotten a haircut. For a moment, that moment, he looked like someone's dad. He turned, barely smiling when he saw her. She held up the picture.

Because it wasn't her baby, it was theirs.

Ryder couldn't remember a time in his life that he'd been this nervous. And he had a pretty good feeling it was only going to get worse. For over an hour he'd been watching other women, other couples. A few couples had new babies with them.

That was going to be his life. Andie was going to get a round belly. She would need help getting up from a chair, like a couple of the women who were obviously farther along. Their husbands had helped them up, and held their hands as they walked back to the examining rooms.

He'd never seen himself as one of those men. Man, he'd never even seen himself standing next to a woman, not in his craziest dreams.

He didn't even know how to hold a baby.

Andie walked toward him, her cheeks flushed and that picture in her hand. He'd never seen her so unsure. At least he wasn't alone in his feelings.

"This is our baby." She handed him the picture. In a few months she wouldn't be wearing jeans. He tried to picture her in maternity clothes, pastel colors and with her feet swollen.

She'd hit him if she knew what direction his

thoughts were taking. If she knew that he'd been thinking about being there when the baby was born and what they'd name it.

"Is it a boy or a girl?" He held the picture up and tried to decipher the dot that she insisted was their kid. "Are you sure that's a baby? Looks like a tadpole to me."

She laughed. "That's a baby. And we won't know what it is for a few months."

"Wow." He shook his head and looked at the picture again. "We're going to be parents."

"Yeah, we are."

It became real at that moment, with her next to him in a doctor's office. Andie was going to have his baby.

He slipped his arm around her waist and pulled her close, because how could he not. It felt like what a guy had to do when he found out he was going to be a dad. He hadn't expected it, that jolt of excitement, that paternal surge of protectiveness.

Five minutes ago he'd been full of regrets, full of fear, full of doubt. He still was, but a picture of a heart beating, that had to change something.

"Stop." Andie pulled loose. "You're making me nervous."

"Sorry."

"I forgive you, but you have to feed me."

He got it. And he had to stop acting like she

was someone other than Andie. He wondered how they did that, how they acted like they had acted for the past twenty-five years.

"When do we come back?" He asked as they walked out the doors of the clinic, into warm autumn sunshine.

"We don't. I visit Dr. Ashford in a month. She's at the Lakeside Women's Clinic."

"I want to go with you."

"Ryder, please stop. You don't have to do this."

He stopped walking. People moved past them and around them. Andie kept moving so he hurried to catch up with her, to walk across the parking lot at her side.

"I don't know why you're pushing me away." He pulled the keys out of his pocket and pushed the button. "Andie, we have to face this. It isn't going away."

"I know it isn't going away. But I don't want to feel like you're tied to me, knowing you'd rather be anywhere but here. This isn't who you are. This isn't who we are."

"Who are we then?"

"You're you. You're single and you love your life. And I ride barrel horses and live with my granny. That's our lives. This, having a baby, being parents together, this isn't us."

He didn't laugh at her because he'd been

reading those magazines in the waiting room and he now knew all about hormones, estrogen, cravings and labor. A few months ago those had been words he wouldn't have even thought to himself. He thought he might have information overload, received after more than an hour of reading prenatal articles.

Stretch marks, whether to medicate during labor or not, natural delivery verses C-section. He wanted the words to go away.

Anyway, he knew better than to laugh at a pregnant woman with surging hormones. She'd either cry hysterically or hurt him. And he wasn't much into either of those options.

He wasn't about to tell her that he'd much rather be at a rodeo than facing her right then. At least he knew what to expect at a rodeo, on the back of a horse, or on the back of a bull. For the time being he had to think that those days were behind him.

That meant he had to come up with something that would placate her until they could deal with this.

Cravings. The word was now his friend.

"What do you want to eat?"

Her blue eyes melted a little and she sniffled. He didn't have a handkerchief.

"Seafood."

"You got it."

That was a lot easier than dealing with the big changes happening in his life, and her body. He shuddered again as he opened the door for her to get into the truck.

As they drove through Tulsa, he glanced at the woman sitting next to him. The mother of his child. He'd never expected her to be that.

"Andie, we're going to have to talk about this."

"This?"

He sighed. "The baby. Our baby. We have to talk about my part in this."

Her hand went to her belly and she stared out the window. He didn't know if she even realized that she did that, that she touched her belly. He glanced sideways, catching her reflection in the glass. Blue eyes, staring out at the passing buildings and her bottom lip held between her teeth.

"Yeah, I know that we need to talk." She said it without looking at him. "But not yet. Let this settle, okay? Let me get it together and then we'll talk."

"Tomorrow, then, Andie. We'll talk tomorrow." About the future. About them. And about the ring he was still carrying in the pocket of his jeans.

Not that he was planning on proposing again anytime soon. One rejection a year was probably more than enough.

* * *

Andie breathed a sigh of relief as she sat down to lunch. It was officially the "tomorrow" that Ryder had talked about yesterday, and he hadn't shown up yet. She'd managed to get a lot of work done at the barn, found her favorite cow just after she'd calved. The new calf had been standing behind her, still a little damp and a little wobbly.

She'd managed to forget, for a few hours, how drastically her life would change next spring.

What Ryder needed to do was go back on the road, rope a few steer, or help Wyatt with the girls. He had to get over thinking she'd let him marry her just because. When she thought about that, about marrying Ryder, her heart didn't know how to react.

She reached for a magazine off the pile sitting on the edge of the table expecting *Quarter Horse Monthly,* and she got lace and froth instead. One of Alyson's bridal magazines. Andie picked it up and flipped through the pages. She shuddered and closed the magazine.

"What's up with you?" Etta walked into the kitchen. She smiled and laughed a little. "Weddings make you nervous."

"White icing, white dresses, white fluff and white lace."

"It's a special occasion." Etta sat down across

from her and picked up the magazine. "It's supposed to be white and frilly. It's supposed to be unlike any other day in a woman's life."

"Right, but couldn't it be white denim and apple pie with vanilla ice cream?"

"I guess it could, if that's what the bride wanted. Are you thinking of getting married?"

"Of course not. Who would I marry? And there definitely isn't any white in my future."

Andie flipped the magazine open and a strange feeling, something like longing—if she'd been giving it a name—ached inside her heart. In high school her friends had planned their weddings. They'd planned the dresses, the flowers, the reception, even the groom and where they'd go on their honeymoon.

Not Andie. She'd saved up farm money to buy the barrel horse of her dreams and the perfect saddle. She'd planned a National Championship win, and she had the buckle to show how well she'd planned.

Etta patted her hand. "You'll have a white wedding, Andie. My goodness, girl, you know that it isn't about what you've done. It's about what God's doing in your heart. This is about the changes that have taken place in your life."

"I know." What else could she say? It wasn't about white. But then again, it was. It was also about dreams she'd never dreamed. "I need to get back to work. What's for dinner tonight? I wouldn't mind taking you out for supper at the Mad Cow."

"I'd love it. I have an order to ship off this afternoon." Tie-dye specialties, Etta's custom clothing line. She and Andie worked together when Andie wasn't on the road.

"Do you need help getting the order together?"

"No, you go ahead with what you need to get done."

Andie took her plate to the sink and walked out the back door. The weather had turned cool and the leaves were rustling in a light breeze. She walked down the path to the barn, whistling for her horses. They were a short distance away and her whistle brought their heads up. Their ears twitched and then they went back to grazing.

Dusty left the herd and started toward the barn. She would brush him first and work him a little. No need to let him get a grass belly. No reason for her to sit and get lazy, either. She'd never been good at sitting still.

For as long as she could remember she'd ridden horses. When she turned six, her dad bought Bell, a spotted pony. That summer she had started to compete in youth rodeos around Oklahoma and Texas. And she'd been competing ever since. For over twenty years.

But this next year would bring changes. She'd seen the women on the circuit with children. But they usually had husbands, too. And they didn't drag little babies from state to state.

Life's about changing—those words were in a song Etta liked.

She snapped a lead rope on Dusty's halter and led him into the barn where she tied him to a hook on the wall. He rubbed his head on the rough wood of the barn and tried to chew on the rail of the nearest stall while she brushed him and then settled the saddle on his back. She reached under his belly and grabbed the girth strap to pull it tight.

A few minutes later she was standing in the center of the arena with her horse on a long, lunge line. This was what she loved. She loved an autumn day and a horse that was so attentive it took barely a flick of her wrist or a slight whistle to command him.

Ryder pulled up the drive as she was settling into the saddle. Not that long ago she would have rode to the fence, glad to see him. But today wasn't three months ago. She blinked away a few tears and she didn't glance in his direction, but she knew he was parking, that he was getting out of his truck.

She rode Dusty around the arena, keeping close to the fence. He was restless and wanted his head, kept pulling, wanting her to let him go. She held him in, easing him from an easy canter to a walk and then she rode him into the center of the arena, taking him in tight circles. He obeyed but she knew what he really wanted were barrels to run.

As she headed back to the fence she made brief eye contact with Ryder. He was walking toward the arena looking casual, relaxed, but even from a distance she saw his jaw clench.

"What are you doing?" He opened the gate and stepped inside the arena.

"I'm working my horse."

"Really?"

"Really." She reined Dusty in, and he didn't want to be reined in. He pranced, fighting the bit, wanting to run.

When he realized it was time to work, he was always ready to go. She held him back though, as her attention settled on Ryder. The new Ryder.

He still looked like the old Ryder. Her gaze traveled down from his white cowboy hat to his face shadowed and needing a shave, and then to the T-shirt and faded jeans. He'd tanned to a deep brown over the summer and in the last few years his body had changed from that of a tall skinny teen to a man who worked cattle for a living.

He had changed. This Ryder didn't seem to get her. Or maybe he wanted to change her? He shook his head and walked toward her and the horse.

"I don't think you should do this."

"Why not?" She held the reins tight and patted Dusty's neck, whispering softly to calm the animal.

"You're pregnant."

"I think I know that." She glared at him, hoping to pin him down, back him off, or make him turn tail and run. He crossed his arms in front of his chest, like he was the law and she was the errant juvenile. He'd never been one to back down from a fight.

Had she really admired that about him?

"Seriously, Andie, you can't do this. It's dangerous."

"No, it isn't. The doctor said I could ride. He said I could do what I've been doing, within reason. I've got to exercise my horse. I can't let him get out of shape. And I'm not going to get hurt."

"Fine, but I'm going to stay here and watch."

"Like I need you to stay and watch. You have better things to do with your time than be my nanny."

"Yeah, I have better things to do, but if you insist on doing this, then I'm staying here."

She pushed her hat back and tried again to stare him down. "This doesn't make you my keeper. We're not boyfriend and girlfriend. We're not going steady."

"You're right, because we're not sixteen. This is a whole lot more than going steady. This is having a baby."

"Like I need you to tell me." She closed her eyes, because they did sound like kids. She didn't want that.

Ryder stepped closer. "I don't want to fight with you."

She really didn't like change.

"I don't want to fight, either. We've never fought before."

He looked away, but his hand was still on Dusty's neck. He let out a sigh. "I'm sorry."

"You have to stop this." She backed her horse, away from Ryder because she had to take back control, of herself and her horse. "You have to stop treating me this way, like I'm going to break."

"I'm trying." His features softened a little and he smiled, a shy smile that was almost as out of place as this new, protective behavior of his.

It was sweet, that smile and her insides warmed a little. She nudged Dusty with her boots and he stepped forward, putting Ryder next to her again.

"Ryder you have to trust that I'm not going to do something dangerous. I won't put—" she stumbled over the words "—I won't put our baby in danger."

"I know you won't. This is just new territory for me. I've never been anyone's dad. I hadn't planned on it."

"That makes two of us. I hadn't planned on being anyone's mom, not like this." She slid off the back of her horse. "So, what are you doing here so early?"

He looked a little blank, as if he didn't have a real answer. Maybe he wasn't sure why he was there. They were both experiencing a lot of that lately.

She was experiencing it at that very moment, because she wanted him to say things, about them, about the future. And she knew that wasn't them, it wasn't who they'd ever been.

And it shouldn't hurt, knowing those weren't the words he was going to say. He was probably there just to check up on her and nothing more.

She wouldn't let it bother her. She knew what to do—turn and walk away, the way she would have a few months earlier. But nope, she stood there waiting for him to suddenly say the right thing.

Chapter Seven

What was he doing there? Ryder had asked himself that question a few times on the drive over to Andie's. In all the years he'd known her, he'd never had to ask himself that question.

Okay, once, but that's because he'd kissed her the night of her senior prom, a night when she'd decided it would be easier to go with him than to worry about having a date. So he'd headed home from college in Tulsa to be her date.

He laughed a little, thinking back to the two of them in the limo his dad had hired for the night. They'd taken a half dozen of their friends along for the ride and when he'd walked her to the front door at the end of the night, knowing Etta was inside watching, he'd kissed Andie.

The next day they'd made a promise never to complicate their relationship that way again. Their reasons had been good. If a relationship went bad, they knew they wouldn't be able to go back to being just friends. They'd kept that promise until that night when she'd looked vulnerable and he hadn't listened to his good sense and walked away.

He was here now because they were going to have a baby together and they needed to be able to be parents together. So it seemed as if working on a relationship was the best way to start the process. Especially if she was just going to laugh when he handed her a ring and proposed.

Wyatt had laughed, too. No matter what the situation, a woman wanted more from a proposal than some half-hearted attempt at being romantic. Ryder got a little itchy under the collar when he thought about romance in connection with Andie.

"Ryder, what is it you wanted to do?"

"I thought maybe we could go over to the Coopers' arena tonight. A few people are going to get together, buck out some bulls, rope some steers and maybe run barrels."

"You'd let me run barrels?" She grinned and he shuffled his feet and looked away, because her running barrels on Dusty was the last thing he wanted.

"I can't stop you." He stepped back from her horse.

"No, you can't."

She smiled at him, and he knew she was pushing, messing with him. That smile took him back. It was easy to remember being kids, chasing down some dirt road outside of Dawson, doing stuff kids did in the country because going out on real dates took money and a town other than the one they lived in.

They'd built bonfires and sat in groups. Sometimes they found a parking lot in Dawson and parked in a circle, sitting on the tailgates of pickup trucks. In the summer they'd gone to the lake or skiing.

Sometimes the two had dated, but never each other. Andie had dated Reese Cooper. And today that bothered him.

Life had been a lot simpler twelve years ago. But they'd been kids, and kids didn't think about what the future held. When Wyatt had met Wendy in college, he'd never dreamed of losing her too soon. He'd dreamed of having her forever. They'd planned to be youth leaders in a church and save the world.

The irony of that twisted in Ryder's gut and he knew Wyatt had to feel a lot more twisted up over losing his wife. What Ryder wouldn't give to go back to sitting in the parking lot of the Mad Cow with a bunch of kids who had nothing more serious to talk about than the rodeo that weekend and what events they would enter.

"You look like a guy that took a bitter pill," Andie teased as she led her horse through the gate he'd opened.

"Just thinking back." And thinking ahead.

"Yeah, we had some good times, didn't we?"

"We did." He walked on the other side of Dusty, but he peeked over the horse's back to look at Andie. He'd give anything to put a smile back on her face, to make her stop worrying.

"It isn't the end of the world, Ryder."

"I know it isn't." He even managed to laugh. "I'm not sixteen, Andie. When I looked in the mirror this morning, that fact was pretty evident. Most of the people we went to school with have been married for years and have a few kids."

"We're not getting married."

She tied the horse and Ryder slid his hand down the animal's rump, ignoring the tail that switched at flies and a hoof that stomped the dirt floor of the barn. He rounded the horse to the side Andie stood on. She was already untying the girth strap.

"So, do you want to go with me?" He lifted the saddle off the horse's back and ignored the sharp look she gave him.

He opened the door of the tack room with his foot and walked inside the dark room. The light came on. He glanced over his shoulder at Andie standing in the doorway. She watched as he dropped the saddle on the stand and hung the bridle on the wall. When he turned around, she was still watching.

"Well?" He followed her out of the room, latching the door behind him.

"Yeah, sure, I'll go. I haven't seen the Coopers in a long time." She untied Dusty's lead rope and led him out the back door of the barn. "When do we leave?"

"I have to run home and get a few things done. I'll pick you up at five." He was buying more cattle and a quarter horse with blood lines that would ramp up his herd.

"I'll be ready."

He nodded and for a moment he was tempted, really tempted to kiss her goodbye, to see what it would feel like if they were a couple. Common sense prevailed because he knew how it would feel to get knocked to the ground if he pushed too far too fast.

Instead he touched her arm and walked to the truck that he'd left idling in her driveway thirty minutes earlier. He climbed inside feeling like a crazy fool. When had he ever been the guy who didn't know what to say? He'd been that person a lot lately.

When he first got there, they hadn't been able to carry on a conversation. She had even questioned why they were fighting. He had an answer for that. Couples fought. He didn't want that to be his future with Andie. Their future.

He backed down her driveway, looking into the rearview mirror at what was behind him. Behind him, that was familiar territory. What was ahead, that was a whole other matter.

Kat and Molly were playing in his yard when he pulled up to the house a few minutes later. Cute kids, still smiling, still able to chase butterflies and blow seed puffs off the dandelions. When he thought about what they'd been through, what Wyatt had been through, he felt like an idiot for crying over his own spilled milk.

Man, life was tough sometimes. Real tough.

Wyatt was leaning against a tree watching the girls, watching Ryder pull up. He waved and stepped away from the tree. As Ryder got out of his truck, Wyatt was there, smiling a little more than he had a few days ago.

How would a guy ever smile again if he'd lost someone like Wendy?

"Some girl named Sheila called." Wyatt watched the girls, but he managed to shoot Ryder a knowing look. "Told her I'd take a message but she said she'd left messages and you hadn't called her back."

"Yeah, I'll call her in a few days. You getting settled in okay?"

"Yeah, you getting in trouble with the women?

I think there was a call from someone named Anna, too. She left a message on the answering machine."

"I'll call her, too."

"Keeping them on a stringer?"

"They aren't fish."

"No, but you sure know how to haul them in like they are."

Ryder shoved his hands into his pockets and bit back about a dozen things he'd like to say to his older brother. Wyatt had always made all the right decisions. Wyatt had stayed in church, because he said it wasn't God's fault that people messed up sometimes.

In Ryder's opinion, people messed up a little more often than sometimes.

"Ryder, if you need to talk?"

Right, lay his problems on Wyatt's shoulders when Wyatt couldn't see through his grief to raise two little girls who were still laughing, still smiling. They were chasing a kitten and giggling, the sound picking up in the wind and carrying like the seeds from the dandelion that they'd picked.

"Why do you think I need to talk?"

Wyatt shrugged. "I don't know, just a hunch. You're ignoring women. And you're buying cattle."

"Right."

He was growing up and everyone was surprised. That itched inside him a little. Couldn't he do a mature thing without people getting suspicious? He guessed the answer had to be no.

"Everyone in town still going to the Dawson Community Church?" Wyatt leaned to pick up Kat who had run across the yard to him and was lifting her arms to be held.

"Yeah, I suppose most do."

"You want to go with us on Sunday?"

"No, not really." Ryder rubbed his jaw and shot Wyatt a look. He might as well get it together now. "Yeah, I guess."

Wyatt whistled. "This must be big."

Big. He knew what Wyatt meant. Something big had to happen for Ryder to be thinking about church. So, that's what people thought about him, that he was only going to have faith if God somehow pushed him into it with a big old crisis.

He pulled at his collar because it was tight and the sun was hitting full force now. It shouldn't be this warm at this time of year, just days away from October.

"So?" Wyatt pushed, his gaze darting beyond Ryder to focus on his daughters. Ryder turned to look at the girls. They'd caught the kitten.

"Yeah, it is something big." Ryder picked up a walnut and tossed it. "Andie's going to have a baby and I'm the dad."

It was a long moment and then Wyatt whistled, the way he'd whistled years ago when Ryder was fifteen and had managed to talk a senior girl into taking him to the prom. But it wasn't anything like admiration in his eyes this time. Wyatt shook his head, and he looked kind of disgusted.

"How'd that…?"

"Don't ask. It was a mistake."

"Or something like it." Wyatt watched his girls play and he shook his head again. "Man, Ryder, I just don't know what to say."

Ryder guessed congratulations were out of the question, so he shrugged. "Not much you can say."

"You going to marry her?"

"That makes us sound like we're sixteen."

"You're not sixteen by a lot of years, but she's having your baby and you've loved her since she stepped on the bus her first day of kindergarten and pushed you out of her seat."

"You can't claim a seat on your first day of school, and I had seniority." He smiled at the memory of a little girl with blond pigtails and big eyes. She'd been madder than an old hen at him. She'd been that mad more than once in the past twenty-five years.

"So, marry her, have a family together."

"We're best friends. That isn't love. And she said no."

"She turned you down?"

"Yeah." He laughed a little. "She turned me down."

A smart guy would have let it go. Especially a guy who had always been pretty happy being single. Instead of letting it go, he'd invited her to go to the Coopers'. They had always gone together.

Tonight, though, it was a date. Tonight it was step one in him convincing her to say yes to his next proposal. A couple having a baby should get married.

He repeated that to his brother and Wyatt shook his head.

"Really, Ryder, you think that's the best line to use when proposing?"

"What am I supposed to say? She's Andie."

"Right, she's Andie. But no matter what, she's a woman. Maybe it's time you realized that and started treating her like one, instead of acting like she's one of the guys."

Andie, a woman? It seemed like a good time to end the conversation. He knew Andie well enough to know she didn't want him to start treating her like a girl. She definitely wouldn't want romance and flowery words.

She was Andie. He thought he knew a little something about what she liked and didn't like.

* * *

Andie walked into the kitchen and glanced at the clock. That was the last thing she wanted to do, check the time again. She'd been doing that all afternoon, almost as if she had a date.

Ryder wasn't a date.

She walked to the back door and leaned against the wall to shove her foot into one boot, and then the other. She didn't bother to untuck her jeans.

"I think this is a good idea." Etta stood at the kitchen sink. She dried a plate, put it in the cabinet and turned to face Andie.

Andie couldn't agree on the "good idea" part. How could it be a good idea, for her to show up with Ryder, making the two of them look like a couple?

"What?" Etta poured herself a cup of coffee and held it between her hands, watching Andie.

Okay, she must have made a face of some kind or Etta wouldn't be asking "What?"

Andie met her grandmother's serious gaze, felt the warmth of a smile that had been encouraging her for as long as she could remember.

"Everyone is going to know." Okay, it sounded ridiculous when she said it like that. "That sounds crazy, doesn't it?"

Etta shrugged, her big silver hoop earrings jangling a little. "Oh, maybe it sounds a little ridiculous. I was going to say that you're not fifteen, but I don't think it matters. You're having a baby. You're going to have to face that and face people. I promise you aren't going to be able to hide the fact."

"I know that."

"So, go with Ryder and make the best of things. Make the best of your relationship because that baby deserves for the two of you to act like grown-ups."

"We're working on it."

"I know you are. And Andie, I know you're working on having faith. I want you to remember that even if folks talk a little, even if they gossip, things will work out and your friends are going to stick by your side." Etta smiled. "And I would imagine even the ones gossiping will stick by you, once they get it out of their system."

"Thanks, Gran." She hugged Etta tight and then Ryder was knocking on the door. "Time to go."

"Have fun," Etta called out as Andie went out the back door.

Ryder stepped away from the porch rail he was leaning against and tipped his hat back as she walked out the door. She paused, for just a breath of a second and then let the door close behind her. He even reached out his hand for hers. But she couldn't go there, not yet. She wasn't quite ready for this new relationship, or the new Ryder.

A year ago if he'd grinned and winked at her, she would have told him to peddle his charms somewhere else, to some other female. She walked down the steps and Ryder followed, catching up and walking next to her.

"This is supposed to be a date." Ryder pushed the door of the truck closed when she tried to open it. She glared and he smiled.

"I wanted to open the door for you," he murmured.

"You don't have to. It looks as if you already loaded my horse." Back up, slow down. She took in a deep breath. "Ryder, I've seen you on dates, I know that side of you, the guy who charms and courts. I don't want that. I want my best friend."

"I am your best friend."

"But that guy never opened the door for me. He also didn't try to hold my hand."

"I guess that's the truth." He looked down at the ground and then back up, his dark eyes hanging on to hers. "Do you know how to go back?"

The words bounced between them like a game of pinball gone bad. They just stood there, facing each other and facing reality. And Andie finally closed her eyes and shook her head.

He pulled the truck door open and motioned for her to get in. Andie sat down in the leather bucket seat and Ryder leaned, close enough for her to catch the scent of his soap and to notice that the hair curling under his hat was still damp. She reached, nearly touching those soft curls at the nape of his neck. But she couldn't make that connection because thinking about it stole her breath and made her thoughts turn to being held by him.

That was a lot more complicated than holding his hand.

Ryder backed away, as if his own thoughts troubled him more than he could admit. He winked and closed the truck door.

They rode in silence to the Circle C Ranch, which was owned by the Cooper family. George Strait played on the radio and the breeze whipped in through open windows. Andie loved autumn, had always looked forward to the changing temperatures, the leaves turning colors and the scent of smoke from fireplaces and woodstoves.

This year she looked forward to surviving, to getting past this moment and finding the next path of her future. With a child. She watched out the window, spotting a fox chasing across the field. It distracted her, but just for a moment and then her thoughts went back again.

To faith.

Faith. She closed her eyes and tried to dig up the tattered remnants of what had felt like faith two months ago, before she knew. She'd been seeking a new beginning, thinking she could work it all out, that she'd suddenly not be angry with her mother and that she would immediately forgive. Instead, she was facing a totally different set of problems.

She didn't want her baby to grow up feeling like a problem.

She wouldn't let that happen.

"Cheer up, Andie, we'll get through this." Ryder's easy comment, said with a smile.

"Of course we will." She kept her gaze on the window, at the fields and neighboring farms.

"Or we'll give up, sing about gloom, despair and agony on us, and cry in our oatmeal?"

"Stop being an optimist." She turned up the radio, refusing to smile.

Ryder turned it back down. They were on the long drive that led to the Coopers'. A dozen or more trucks and trailers were parked in a gravel area to the south of the arena and people milled around, leading horses or standing in groups talking.

"I'm going to be an optimist, Andie." Ryder slowed the truck and parked. "I'm going to be the person you count on. I might not pull it off without a hitch, but I'm going to do my best."

"Okay, we'll try this out." She reached for the

truck door. "But don't get creepy on me. I want to know that some things haven't changed."

But she knew better. They both knew better.

When they got out of the truck, he met her at the back of the trailer and she could tell that he had more to say. He held onto the latch of the trailer gate, looking inside at their horses.

"Listen, Andie, we've been through a lot together." He pulled up on the latch. "We went through the mess of my pretty dysfunctional family and you stood by me. We were kids, spitting on our hands and shaking, making a deal to forget about church because of what happened."

"It was wrong."

"I know, but it happened and my dad was the reason it happened. I've been thinking a lot about faith, and church. I've been thinking that maybe we should hang tight, stick this out together."

"This, you mean the pregnancy?"

He turned red. "Yeah, the pregnancy."

"You can barely say it."

"I can say it. And I can tell you that on Sunday I'll be picking you up for church."

"I'm holding you to that. But why now?"

"Because I'm not going to be my dad. This kid isn't going to have to worry about what his parents are doing or how messed up his family is."

"It could be a girl."

"I'm okay with a girl."

"That's good, because I think it is a girl." Andie couldn't look at Ryder, not when they were talking about their baby, their future. But they weren't discussing marriage because he didn't love her and she wouldn't marry someone who didn't love her.

What if someday he really fell in love with someone, someone he wanted to marry? What then? Or what if she fell in love? She met his gaze, those dark eyes that she knew so well, eyes she had looked into a thousand times before.

What if she lost him as a friend? She had protected that friendship for years. How did she protect it now, when they were facing the biggest challenge of their lives?

"We should go." He opened the gate and she backed up. "Andie, I mean it. I know my track record is pretty shaky, but I'm in this for the long haul."

Lights came on around the arena and someone whooped out a warning for them to hurry.

"I know you are," she whispered.

Or at least she wanted to hope. But she couldn't dwell on that. This moment, facing friends, people they'd known their whole lives, was going to take all the courage she could muster.

For a brief second his fingers touched hers, grasping them lightly and then letting go. She tried not to think about high school, about how everything had been a new experience and holding hands had been more about belonging to someone and less about really being in love.

And belonging was okay.

He stepped into the trailer and backed her horse out. She took the lead rope and moved out of his way as he backed his horse out.

"Is it too late to change our minds?" She glanced up at him and he smiled.

"I think this is pretty permanent."

"I don't mean about the baby, you goof. I mean about this, about facing people, facing questions."

"I think it's too late. We're okay, Andie."

That was easy for him to say. She'd never felt less okay in her life. But he was getting their horses out of the trailer and if she was going to live her life in Dawson, she would have to deal with looks and whispers.

Ryder tightened the girth strap on his saddle and the big roan gelding that he'd brought with him twitched and stomped his back hooves. The roan was new and Ryder couldn't even get used to the horse's name. Half the time he couldn't remember it. But the name Red worked and the horse didn't seem to care.

"I'm going to tie Dusty and head over to the

arena." Andie smiled but he didn't think the look met up with her eyes the way it should.

But he didn't question her. He wasn't going to start doing that. He was the baby's dad, not Andie's keeper. He was having a hard time keeping those two things separate.

"Okay. They're going to put out the barrels later. After steer wrestling and team roping."

"I know, but I'm not sure if I'll ride him tonight. These are younger riders with younger horses. I'll just give pointers if they want, but…"

"Not be a show-off."

She smiled, this time it looked like the real thing. "Yeah, something like that."

Someone yelled his name. "Gotta run."

She nodded and he almost didn't go. But he had to ride away, to keep this moment normal. He grabbed the saddle horn and swung into the saddle, nearly reaching for her hand and pulling her up with him once he was in the saddle. Instead he held tight to the reins and backed away.

But she hadn't moved. He nudged the red roan forward, close to her and she looked up, questions in her eyes. He didn't have a single answer for her. Instead he leaned and touched her cheek.

"I won't let you down."

She nodded and he rode off, leaving her there alone.

When he got to the arena Reese Cooper motioned him forward.

"You gonna rope with Clay tonight?"

Ryder nodded. "If he needs a partner, I'm the guy."

"He thought so." Reese Cooper was one of the middle Cooper kids. And there were a few of them. Ryder had lost track but he thought there were more than a dozen kids in the Cooper clan. Some were biological, some adopted and a few were foster kids that stayed.

Clay was adopted from Russia years ago. Five years ago he hit about sixteen and every girl in Dawson went crazy over him.

Reese had always been the center of attention.

Ryder wasn't bothered by the fact that the ladies loved the Cooper clan. It meant he could live his life without too many problems from the ladies of Dawson. It did kind of bother him that Andie had dated Reese.

"You gonna ride a bull tonight?" Clay walked up, sandy blond hair and gray eyes. His chaps were bright pink, because Clay didn't care what anyone thought of pink.

"I've thought about it." Ryder settled into the saddle of the roan gelding, holding him steady because the horse hadn't adjusted yet. Obviously the animal had led a quiet life up to this point.

Tonight was a real test for him, what with lights, noise and a few rangy bulls bellowing from the pens to the side of the arena.

"Come on, then, we've got bulls ready." Clay spoke with an accent. Ryder tried not to smile because he hadn't figured out if the accent was real, or just something he used as a gimmick. It just seemed that when the kid had been ten or twelve, the accent hadn't been so thick.

Ryder glanced around the arena, finally spotting Andie. She was sitting on the row of risers with Jenna Cameron and the twins. And Jenna's new baby. Funny, thinking about Jenna married to Adam MacKenzie, retired pro football player, and owner of Camp Hope. Adam and Clint, now brothers-in-law, must have brought the bulls over.

That meant they'd be over by the pens on the opposite side of the arena.

"I'll ride a bull." Ryder backed his horse away from the two Coopers. "I'm going to say hello to Clint and Adam. And when you're ready to rope, let me know."

He rode around the back side of the arena, passing a few friends who waved but didn't stop him for a conversation. They looked at him, though, as if they knew. It wouldn't be long before everyone knew.

Clint and Adam were moving the bulls through

the pens and into the chutes. Clint waved and then closed a gate between two pens.

"Ryder, good to see you here." Adam MacKenzie walked toward him. "I've been meaning to tell you how much I appreciated the help with fences at Camp Hope."

"It was no big deal."

"Seriously, though, it meant a lot to us." Adam pulled a cola out of a cooler and tossed it his way.

"I didn't mind at all. The camp is a great thing for the kids, and for this community. Gives Dawson something to talk about besides…"

Besides him, for a change.

"How was your season?" Clint had joined them. A few years back the two had ridden to events together. Until Willow showed up in town. And Jenna's boys. The two, Clint and Willow, had fallen in love while taking care of Jenna's boys.

Now that Ryder thought about it, all of their lives had been taking some pretty serious direction changes. These guys didn't seem the worse for wear.

Of course for the last couple of years, Ryder had done a lot of teasing. His friends had all fallen, and they'd all changed their ways. They were family men, now. They went to church and took care of their wives and kids.

He hadn't really envied them.

And now they were staring at him, waiting for him to answer Clint's question.

"Good, really good. Brute turned into a great gelding. I don't know if I told you, but I bought his daddy last week. I needed a good stud horse on the place."

"That sounds like a career choice," Adam interjected with a smile.

"Yeah, maybe." He glanced toward the bleachers. He knew where Andie was sitting, even if he couldn't see her clearly from where he was.

"How's Wyatt?" Clint changed the subject and Ryder met his gaze, saw his smile shift. "I saw him drive through town the other day."

Ryder shrugged, and he didn't sit down. "Wyatt's as good as he can be. It's been a long year for him. I don't know how a guy gets over that."

Gets over finding his wife dead and their two little girls in the playpen, crying. How did Ryder convince his brother there were good days ahead? How did he tell Wyatt to have faith, when Ryder had been ignoring God for as long as he could remember?

"Yeah, it won't be easy. But he's got a whole community behind him here." Clint reached for Red's reins. "Want me to hold him while you get your bull rope ready?"

"I guess if I'm going to ride a bull, I'd better get ready. You riding?"

Clint laughed. "No, I don't think so. We've got one little girl and Willow found this little boy in Texas. He's three and hearing impaired."

Ryder nodded because he didn't know what to say. He dismounted and handed Red over to Clint. "You and Willow are pretty amazing."

"Willow's amazing." Clint had hold of the roan and the horse was flighty, more flighty than Ryder liked from a roping horse.

"Ryder, up in two."

Ryder took the bull rope that Adam tossed at him. "Might want to borrow rosin from one of the other guys."

"Got it." Ryder pulled a glove out of his pocket. At least he'd remembered that. As he walked up to the chutes, he didn't look at Andie. Instead he took the Kevlar vest that Clay Cooper offered.

"It's one of Willow's bulls. Think you can handle him?" Clay asked with a grin that didn't do much to impress Ryder. Someone needed to take that guy out back and knock some of that vinegar out of him.

"I think I can handle him." Ryder pulled on the vest.

The bull that came through the chute was a big brindled bull with too much Brahma in its DNA. He didn't like to ride Brahma bulls. Not because they were meaner, bucked harder or went after a guy. He didn't like the hump. It knocked him off balance, made it hard for him to stay up on the bull rope.

As he settled onto the bull's back, Clay snickered, like he'd meant to put Ryder on the worst bull in the pen. He worked rosin into the bull rope and then Clay pulled it, tight, so Ryder could wrap it around his gloved hand.

The bull hunched in the shoot and then went up, front legs off the ground, pawing at the front of the chute. Ryder grabbed the side of the chute and pulled himself up, out of danger. The bull went back down on all fours. They started the bull rope process again.

As soon as Ryder had the rope around his hand and the bull was halfway sane in the chute, he nodded and the gate opened. The bull spun out of the chute, nearly falling and then righting himself. Ryder fell forward but got himself back into position when the bull bucked into his hand. Foam and slobber flew from the bull's head. The force of four hooves hitting the ground jarred his teeth.

He kept forward, his head tucked. The bull jerked him to the side and his body flung off the side of the bull, his hand still in the rope. A few jumps, a few hops and then the buzzer. He jerked his hand loose and rolled.

A bullfighter, another Cooper brother, jumped in front of the bull, giving Ryder a chance to run for his life. That Brahma bull didn't play nice. It was stomping, trying to get his feet, get his legs as he scurried to get away.

As he jumped over the fence, Andie was there. Pale, shaking and pretty darned mad. He'd never seen her like that before. He considered going back in the arena with the bull.

He dropped down on her side of the fence and walked away, dragging the bull rope behind him. She followed. He couldn't do this here with everyone watching, wondering what was going on between them.

When he got to the back of the arena, to a spot where they could talk, he waited.

Andie walked up to him, her blond hair short and blowing in the soft, Oklahoma breeze. The air was dry, but still warm and the sun was starting to set. He didn't know why, but suddenly when he looked at her, he saw someone he hadn't seen before. He saw a woman with soft edges and a look in her eyes that could have sent him running if he hadn't known her better.

They'd gone places together, all of their lives they'd been together. Tonight felt different. Tonight they were one of the couples. He shifted a little and her mouth opened, like she was going to say something, and he was afraid to hear it.

His back hurt and his shoulder throbbed. He didn't need lectures.

"Don't." He shook his head a little and her mouth closed. And he'd hurt her. He hadn't meant to do that. "Not yet, Andie."

Not yet with a rush of female emotions and words, not from Andie. She'd drown him in that stuff and he wouldn't know how to make it work, not with a ton of emotions and hormones hitting him over the head.

He couldn't think like that.

"Fine." She walked away, slim and athletic, but always graceful. He remembered her in a leotard, forced to take ballet because Etta worried that she was too much of a tomboy. She'd hated it, but he remembered going to her one and only recital. She punched him in the gut that day, because he told her she looked pretty.

He watched her walk away. Gut punched. Sometimes she didn't even have to touch him. And every now and then, like right at that moment, he wanted to kiss her again. Even if it landed him on the ground.

Maybe later. He let the idea settle in his mind, even imagined holding her close on Etta's front porch.

"Hey, Andie, come back."

She stopped walking, but she didn't turn to face him. "You said not right now."

"I didn't mean for you to walk away. I meant for you to give me a chance to take a deep breath."

She turned, the wind catching her hair. She held it back with her hand and waited for him to walk up to her.

"I didn't know you were going to ride a bull tonight." She bit down on her bottom lip and looked away from him.

Her dad. He wanted to swear but he didn't. She'd seen her dad broken up a few too many times. She'd always disliked it when he rode bulls, said it brought back too many memories that she'd rather forget.

"I didn't plan on it, but Clay…"

"Pushed you into it?" She shook her head, not buying it.

"Yeah, kind of. I can't believe I let a twenty-one-year-old kid get to me that way."

She wiped his face. "Dirt on your cheek."

"Right." He wiped it again, in case she didn't get it all. And because it was a lot less disturbing when he did it.

"Ryder, would you mind if we went home. I really don't feel like I can do this tonight."

"Yeah, we can go home. Stay here while I get my horse."

* * *

Andie waited for Ryder. When he came toward her on the big roan gelding, she smiled. He rode up close and reached for her hand. She looked up, and he winked. Like old times, she thought. And she needed some old times. She took his hand and he moved his foot, giving her access to the stirrup.

He pulled and she settled behind him, her arms around his waist. The horse sidestepped a few times and then trotted a bumpy trot toward the trailer. Andie didn't mind the trot, not when this was the most normal thing that had happened to her in days.

As they rode past the arena and down the drive toward the trailer, Ryder slowed the horse to a walk. Andie leaned, resting her cheek against his back, against the soft cotton of his shirt. She breathed in deep of his scent and then she felt silly, because it was Ryder.

The horse came to a stop at the trailer, but neither of them moved. Andie didn't want to move, to break the connection between them. Ryder glanced back but he didn't say anything. But his hands touched her hands that were clasped around his middle.

"You okay?"

"I'm good. This is just the most familiar place I've been in a while. You know, riding like this with you. Remember when we used to take your old gelding out at night for long rides."

"Yeah, I remember." His back vibrated with the depth of his voice.

"Those were good times."

"They were. And they aren't behind us, Andie. We're going to have a kid. We can teach him to ride a horse, and to rope a steer."

"Her."

"Right, her." He laughed and she sighed, but then she moved.

Time to leave the familiar for what was real now. "We should go home."

"Give me your hand." He held her hand and she dropped to the ground. "Andie, we'll have more good times."

"I know." She blinked fast to chase away the tears that sneaked up on her.

Ryder landed on the ground next to her. He led the horse back to the trailer and tied it while he pulled off the saddle. Dusty whinnied a greeting because he'd been left behind, tied but not saddled. She untied him and led him to the back of the trailer.

"So, are you okay?" She handed the horse over to Ryder.

"I'll be sore tomorrow. I'm sure everyone will say that I had to leave early because I'm getting soft."

"That's never bothered you before."

"No, and it still doesn't." He led her horse into the trailer. "Go ahead and get in the truck. I'll have them settled and ready to go in a minute."

Andie nodded and she didn't argue. Tonight it was okay to let Ryder do this for her. She climbed into his truck and waited.

A few minutes later he was behind the wheel of the truck and they were easing down the driveway and then turning on to the road that led back to Dawson. It was only minutes before they reached the city limits and tiny Dawson. As they drove past the Mad Cow, Ryder slowed and pulled into the parking lot. There were a half dozen trucks and teenagers sitting on tailgates.

A dozen years ago, they had been the teenagers hanging out in Dawson, not going to Tulsa or Grove on a Friday night because the drive was too far, the gas too expensive. Dating in Dawson had been cheap and easy; hanging out in town, going to a rodeo, or riding practice bulls from a local stock contractor's pen of livestock.

More often than not they ended up somewhere like the Coopers', where it wasn't for prizes or money, just for fun and practice.

Memories piled up and Andie smiled as Ryder parked his truck next to an old Ford. She understood. For a few minutes he wanted to be that kid again, wanted those easier days back. She got out with him and walked to the front of the truck.

One of the kids had set up practice horns at the outside of the circle of trucks. They were farm kids in roper boots, faded jeans and T-shirts, their girlfriends were hanging together on the back of one truck, girls in tank tops and cutoff shorts. Dawson hadn't changed in years.

The boys grouped around Ryder and Andie leaned against his truck to watch, the way she'd watched years ago. But years ago Ryder had flirted and she'd pretended it didn't matter because they were just friends.

"What are you guys up to?" Ryder took the rope that one of the boys held out to him. He ran it through his hands.

"Just hangin' out and practicing up for next weekend. Ag Days is next Saturday and the Junior Championship Rodeo." A tall boy with straw-colored hair and acne spoke up. Andie recognized him as a kid who had moved with his parents to a neighboring farm. "That sure is a nice stud horse you've got now."

Ryder shrugged off the compliment and Andie wanted to ask the questions, about the horse and when he'd gotten it. He'd never bought a horse without telling her.

She'd seen a load of cattle come in, too. The big trailer had hauled the livestock down his driveway and turned them loose in his empty pasture, the one he didn't use for alfalfa. The cattle were there, now, grazing around oil wells that pumped a slow steady stream of crude oil into holding tanks by the road.

Now he was roping fake horns, as if he was going through some kind of midlife crisis. Because of her.

Ryder looped the rope again, swinging, letting it go. It slipped through the air, landing effortlessly on the horns. She remembered watching a few minutes of an outdoor program about fly-fishing in the northern states. There had been a beauty and grace to the casting of the line. Roping, effortlessly the way Ryder did it, had the same grace.

After freeing the rope from the horns, Ryder handed it back to the kid and then gave them a few pointers. He watched as they took turns, and then he gave them more advice.

When had they grown up, she and Ryder? When had they become the older people in town? Andie sighed at the thought of how far, and yet not so far, her life had come from the days of high school.

A dozen years ago Ryder had been one of these kids, under these same bright streetlights on the same dark pavement. Like these kids, he'd been dreaming of the future, dreaming of the best horse, the buckle, the money. No, never the money for Ryder, but winning. He'd always wanted to win. He'd won in basketball and base-ball. He won in the rodeo arena.

As much as he'd won, she knew he'd lost a lot, too. His life hadn't been charmed. His parents had seen to that. And losing them, he still hurt over that loss. She could see the shadows of the pain in his eyes. There were days that he looked like the loneliest guy in the world. He had a quick smile, though. It flashed easily, creating that dimple in his chin. It was disarming, that smile. If a person didn't know better, they'd think he'd never felt pain, never been hurt. She knew better.

Two months ago she had seen the lonely look in his eyes.

A quick cramp in her stomach ended the memories. She drew in a deep breath and fought against the knife-sharp pain. Ryder turned, his eyes narrowed and he didn't say anything. He patted the boy with the straw-colored hair on the shoulder and said he'd be back soon.

As he walked toward her, she saw his fear, felt her own. Fear or relief?

She closed her eyes because she didn't want to know, didn't want to recognize the look in his eyes, or look too deep into her own heart.

"You okay?"

She nodded, because the pain had passed. "Yeah, I'm fine. But I think I'm ready to go home."

Chapter Eight

Sunday morning Ryder pulled his truck up the driveway of Etta's house, fighting a serious case of nerves that matched any that he'd met up with on the back of a bull. He couldn't imagine feeling worse on his wedding day, if he'd ever planned on getting married.

Going to church for the first time in over a dozen years was definitely up there on the list of things that were hard to do.

And that thought pulled his attention off the road and drew it to the glove compartment where he'd tossed the ring that Andie had rejected last week. Last week when he'd thought having a baby meant two people ought to do the right thing and get married. Obviously Andie was of a different mind. And that should have cut him loose, should have sent him back down the road and on his way to a team roping event in Dallas.

Instead he was as determined as ever to prove to Andie that he could be a dad, even if she didn't think he could be a husband. A dad did the right thing, even went to church. He was pretty sure that's what an upstanding dad did. No, he took that back. His own dad had gone to church.

He was going to do better than that.

As he parked, the front door opened. Etta stepped onto the porch, a vision in purple and yellow, a floppy straw hat on her head. She waved with a hand that sparkled with jewelry and went on with the green plastic watering pot, tipping it to water plants that turned her front porch into some kind of crazy jungle.

He was lucky if weeds grew in his flower gardens. At least weeds covered up the bare spaces and had blooms that added some color to the place.

He got out of his truck and walked across the lawn, the grass turning brown, but autumn mums bloomed in the flowerbeds. Etta set her watering can down and waited at the top of the steps. He clunked up the steps, his boots loud on the wood.

"What has you up here so bright and early on a Sunday morning?" Etta grabbed her watering can again and moved to a planter overflowing with purple blooms that he didn't recognize.

"I guess I'm here to go to church." He glanced

off in the direction of the barn, trying to make sense of the crazy turn his life had taken. A calf was mooing and somewhere a dog barked. He wondered if the animals needed to be fed and how much damage Andie would do to him if he did those things for her.

Etta chuckled a little. "You're going to church?"

"Isn't that what you've been telling me to do for the past eighteen years?"

"I guess I have. But why now?"

"Because it's the right thing to do."

"Oh, I see." She headed back into the house, carrying the green watering can. The open door let out the aroma of coffee and something baked with cinnamon. He followed Etta through the door.

"You don't think I should go?" He followed her down the sunlit hallway.

"Of course you should go." She set the can next to the back door and kicked off her slippers. "Grab a cup of coffee and a muffin. Don't take the chocolate chip muffins, those are for our new pastor."

"Gotcha." He walked into the kitchen, always at home here. He didn't have to search for a cup, didn't have to ask where Etta kept the sugar. He'd been a part of this family for as long as he could remember.

But the idea of going to church had settled in the pit of his stomach like old chili. He'd been talked about his entire life. His family had been talked about. His dad had kept the town loaded with reasons to gossip. He should be used to being a conversation piece for the people of Dawson.

He hadn't worked too hard on his own life, to make himself different. He'd dated women whose names he couldn't remember. He'd spent his teen years chased from fields by farmers who didn't want their hay crops ruined by a kid with a four-wheel drive truck.

Now it was different. He sipped the coffee that he'd poured for himself and stood at the sink, looking out the kitchen window. Etta's barn needed to be painted. He sighed and set down his cup.

"What are you here for?"

He turned, bumping his cup but grabbing it before it slid into the sink and spilled. He held it as she walked across the room. He'd never looked at her this way, in the early morning, seeing her as a woman and not his best friend. She'd always been his best friend.

Today she was definitely a woman. Her dark blue dress touched her knees and curved in the right places. Her blond hair framed her face, the color of the dress making her eyes more vivid. Her belly was still flat.

"Don't look at my stomach." She grabbed a cup and poured herself a cup of coffee.

He swallowed more emotions than he could name. She was standing next to him, not looking at him. And she was soft and feminine. She didn't smell like leather. Instead a floral scent floated in the air around her. It swished his way when she moved.

When she turned to look at him, lifting a brow and giving him a look that asked what in the world he thought he was looking at, he shrugged. And he took a step closer. That wasn't a Sunday morning thing to do, stepping closer, sliding his arms around her waist.

She wiggled free and pushed him back.

"Back off, cowboy." She moved to the other side of the kitchen and picked up a muffin.

"You aren't supposed to eat the chocolate chip muffins," he warned.

"Why not?"

"They're for the new pastor."

"Well, I'm pregnant and I'm eating it."

He shrugged again. She'd have to deal with Etta. He watched as she took a few bites, closing her eyes as she chewed. And then there were footsteps on the stairs. Andie's eyes flew open. She grinned, a wicked grin that should have been a warning, and tossed the muffin at him.

He barely caught it, and then Etta walked into the kitchen.

"What are you doing eating those muffins after I told you not to?"

Ryder glanced at Andie and her smile was a little wicked, a little sweet. He had to take the fall for her. "Sorry, I couldn't help myself."

"No, I guess you couldn't. Self-control doesn't seem to be your strongest character trait lately. Well, come on, let's go to church." Etta grabbed the basket of muffins and slid them into a bag. "You can drive."

As they walked out the door, he slid close to Andie. "You owe me."

"I don't think so."

Her voice was soft and her arm brushed his. Everything was changing. Or maybe he hadn't let himself notice before that Andie made everything in his life feel a little better, a little easier.

On the way out the door she paused for a second, closing her eyes and leaning a little toward him.

"Andie, are you okay?"

She nodded. "I'm fine. We need to go or we'll be late."

He hadn't expected to feel this way, as if he needed to protect her, even if he didn't know what to protect her from. But this was the second time in a week he'd seen that look on her face, and the second time he'd felt a stab of fear he hadn't expected to feel.

Andie sat next to Ryder on the third pew from the front of the church. Etta liked to joke that the power of God was down front, so the people in the back were missing out. Andie felt as if the power of two hundred pairs of eyes was in the back and it was all focused on her. And Ryder. It had been eighteen years since they'd been in church together.

His father's actions had pushed them away from God. Her actions had brought them back. Because as much as she'd tried to be angry with God for what had happened to Ryder's dad, she couldn't hide from His presence or her need for this place and faith.

When it had all crumbled in around her, she hadn't wanted to run from God. Instead she'd run to Him. Which is exactly what Etta had always said would happen. And, as Etta liked to remind, she happened to be right most of the time.

"I'd forgotten what it felt like here." Ryder leaned close, his shoulder against hers. She closed her eyes and nodded, because everything hurt too much. Him never loving her hurt. Her stomach hurt. She looked forward, telling herself the pain that had started earlier meant nothing.

"It feels like peace," she whispered, wanting that peace.

"Yeah, that's what it is." Ryder raised his arm and circled her, pulling her closer to his side. The choir sang the closing hymn and Pastor Jeffries smiled out at the congregation. His style of ministry was different than that of Pastor Todd. It was less like a best friend, more like a father.

Final prayer. She needed that prayer. She need for the service to end. As the congregation filed out of their pews, down the aisle, Andie leaned forward, resting her head on the back of the pew in front of her. She took a deep breath and waited for the pain to pass.

"Honey, what's wrong?" Etta's strong voice whispered near her ear. People around her were talking.

"I think I need to leave." She stood up, ignoring Ryder's concern, his hand reaching for hers and Etta standing up behind her. "I have to go."

Panic was shooting through her, making breathing difficult and mixing with the pain that cramped in her lower abdomen. She wiped at tears that slid down her cheeks and tried to smile at the people asking if she was okay, trying to stop her with a cautious hand. Ryder was right behind her, not touching her, but he was there.

As she hurried down the steps of the church toward Ryder's truck, he reached for her arm and pulled her to a stop. Her eyes were blurring with unshed tears and his face hovered close. She wanted to sink into his arms.

"What's wrong?" His voice was hard, but barely above a whisper and his hands held her arms tight, as if she would have escaped. But escape wasn't her plan, not from him, just from the crowds of people in the church, asking questions or staring after her with questions in their eyes.

"I think I need to go to the hospital."

And then Etta was there. Andie drew in a deep breath, breathing past the stress and through the pain. It had been a twinge that morning, but had gotten worse during church.

Etta took her by the arm and led her to the side as people walked past.

"What's wrong?"

Andie drew in another deep breath. "Cramping."

"Then we're definitely going to the hospital." Etta herded them toward Ryder's truck as she talked.

"I don't want to..." *lose my baby.* She couldn't say it.

"Things happen in a pregnancy, Andie. There are different phases and pains. This could be completely normal." Etta pulled the truck door open and motioned for Andie to climb in. "You're going to be fine. The baby is fine."

Andie nodded as she got into the truck, into the seat next to Ryder who was already starting the truck, practically backing out before Etta got the door closed.

"Maybe you could let an old lady get in the truck before you start driving." Etta hooked her seat belt. "Ryder, take a deep breath and just consider this as practice. Lots of unexpected things happen when we have children."

Andie closed her eyes. Prayers slipped through her mind, getting tangled with guilt. Guilt because she shouldn't be having a baby and because, after thinking that she didn't want this, now she was going to ask God to take care of her child?

They drove the thirty minutes to the hospital in twenty. Andie opened her eyes to the flashing lights of an ambulance ahead of them, pulling through the drive in front of the emergency room. This was reality. She touched her stomach and wondered, even though she didn't want to, if she would still be pregnant when she left the hospital.

And if she wasn't... She closed her eyes against the pain that moved to her heart, if she wasn't how would she and Ryder look at one another tomorrow?

Ryder pulled up in front of the door and

stopped. He glanced at her as he turned the truck off, his smile strong, the look in his eyes telling her that everything would be okay. And she was a kid again, worried that her dad wasn't coming home. But Ryder was there. Always there for her.

"We're fine, Andie."

"I know."

He was out of the truck and when she tried to step out next to him, he shook his head and scooped her up. He carried her into the building like she was a little girl with a scraped knee and she tried to tell him she could walk. He shook his head each time she opened her mouth.

"I can walk," she finally managed to say.

"I don't want you to talk."

Etta was next to them, breathing fast as she hurried to keep up with Ryder. "Don't argue. For once in your life, don't argue."

"I'm too heavy." She leaned into his neck and he held her closer, tighter. Her doctor met them at the doors to the E.R. That was the great thing about small towns, and switching to a doctor closer to home.

"What's up, Andie?" Dr. Ashford motioned them into an exam room.

"I've been cramping. It was light at first and I wasn't worried, but today it's worse."

"Okay, let's examine you and see what we can find out."

Ryder practically dumped her on the hospital bed. And then he was gone, the curtain of the exam room flapping behind his exit. Andie shook her head. So much for her hero. Her knight in shining armor. The Lone Ranger. No, wait, that was more like it. The Lone Ranger always rode in to rescue the woman and then hightailed it out of town before he could get too attached.

She couldn't let it bother her. She knew Ryder, knew why he bounced from relationship to relationship. She knew him well enough that she should have known better than to attach even the vaguest of dreams to him.

But then, he had just carried her in here. And she wasn't light.

"Andie, I'm going to do an ultrasound and examine you." Dr. Ashford stood next to the bed. "Do you want someone in here with you?"

Andie shook her head. "I'm a big girl."

But her body trembled from shock as reality set in. She was losing her baby. Ryder being with her wouldn't stop that from happening. And if she was going to fall apart, she wanted to be alone.

Chapter Nine

Ryder paced across the waiting room, again. And then he sat down, again. He felt as if he'd been doing that same thing for hours. It had only been one hour, though. He bristled at the idea of waiting without any recognition of his presence here. He wanted a few answers, at least for someone to tell him Andie was okay.

He'd already asked the receptionist, twice, if she'd find something out for him. Or get someone to give him answers. She'd smiled a pained smile that he thought could have been a little nicer and told him to take a seat and she'd see if she could find something out. He'd watched and she hadn't left her desk or picked up the phone.

Etta grabbed his arm when he started to stand up again.

"If you bother that receptionist or pace across this floor one more time, I'm going to knock you down," she whispered. And he was pretty sure she meant it.

She had a magazine in her hand, rolled up. He hadn't seen her open it and read. She kept picking up magazines, flipping through pages and then putting them down. She wasn't much better off than he was, but he wasn't about to point that out to her.

"Well, what am I supposed to do? I can't go back there. No one will tell me what's going on. What else can I do but pace?"

"Sit there and pray."

"Pray?" He drew in a deep breath and brushed his hand over his face. How much was God wanting to hear from him?

"Yes, pray. What else are you going to do in this situation?"

"I guess you're right." It wasn't like he'd ever stopped believing, he'd just had a hard time with church after what happened with his dad. Something like that left a bad taste in a guy's mouth.

The door to the emergency room opened and the doctor walked across the room, smiling. "You can see her now."

"How is she?" Ryder stood up.

"I'm afraid I can't discuss that with you."

"What?" He growled the question, hadn't meant to, but it roared out of him, causing a few people to glance their way.

"I'm Andie's doctor and she has a right to privacy. But you can go back and see her."

He shook his head as he moved past the doctor, past the receptionist's desk and through the door that opened as he got closer. Anger had boiled up inside him, more anger than he'd felt in a long time. He tried to tamp it back down, to get control before he faced Andie. It wasn't her fault.

It wasn't even the fault of that smug-faced receptionist.

"Ryder, calm down." Etta followed him and for the first time, he couldn't listen, couldn't take her advice.

His gut had been tied up in knots and fear had shoved common sense out the door. Fear and a really healthy dose of anger were now tied together in a pretty untidy package.

He pushed back the curtain of the exam room, ready to let Andie know how he felt about not being included in the list of people who had a right to know how she was. He shouldn't have to remind her that this was his baby, too.

When he saw her, he couldn't speak. He couldn't do anything when faced with the reality of Andie curled on her side, the blue of a hospital gown over her shoulders and the white blanket up to her chin. He waited at the foot of her bed and Etta walked into the room. Etta looked at the monitors, looked at Ryder and then took a seat on the edge of the bed. She hitched her yellow purse over her shoulder and sat there for a minute.

"How are you, sugar bug?" Etta patted Andie's shoulder.

Ryder had wanted to do that. He had wanted to offer words of comfort. He hadn't known how. That was Etta's job. Besides that, he didn't know how to comfort when he was the reason she was here. He was the reason she was hurting.

And she didn't want him to know what was going on.

He wanted to throw something. Instead he shoved his hat a little tighter down on his head and waited for Andie to say something, anything.

He'd never seen her so quiet. Never.

"I'm fine." Andie reached up to pat her granny's hand. "The baby..." She wiped her hand across her face. "I still have a baby."

Ryder closed his eyes and said a big "Thank you." That's how two weeks could change the way a guy thought about life. A man could go from living for himself, to being willing to give up everything to keep a baby safe.

On the way to the hospital, he'd had to turn off the radio. A Tim McGraw song about a man on his knees, begging God to "not take the girl" had come on. He and Andie hadn't been able to look at each other, or talk about it. Ryder had turned the song off and Andie had whispered "Thank you."

"What did the doctor say?" Etta smoothed the blankets and waited, patiently. But Ryder knew Etta. He knew patience was something she could show, but he knew on the inside she was ready to push down walls to get answers and get something done.

"Time will tell." Andie whispered the words and her shoulders shook. Ryder started to move forward, but Etta was way more qualified than he was to handle this situation.

"Well, time does have a way of doing that."

"I don't want to lose my baby." Andie turned, pulling the blanket up, avoiding looking at him. Her eyes were puffy and red and her blond hair tangled around her face, sticking to tear-stained cheeks.

When she'd lost her dad he'd been the one to hold her. They had always held each other. And now she was avoiding looking at him. Awkward had never been a part of their relationship.

Until now. And it scared the life out of him. He'd made a pretty good show of never needing anyone. And all that time he'd been lying to himself, because he needed Andie. He needed her because she was the most consistent thing in his life.

There were probably other reasons. He knew

there were, but right now he couldn't put it all together. He just knew that she had to be safe. She had to be okay. And it wasn't just about the baby.

"I know you don't want to lose this baby." Etta smoothed the hair from Andie's face, as if she was fifteen, not twenty-eight.

Andie sobbed again, shuddering. "I didn't want this baby. This isn't how I would want my child's life to start. This isn't the way a child wants to grow up thinking about itself. But now... Now I can't stand the idea of losing it, of losing my baby."

Their baby. Ryder almost said something, but he bit back the words. He was definitely not experienced at female emotions. He was used to the Andie that threw rocks in the creek and could break about the rankest horses in the county. She knew how to hang on tight through some wild rides. He'd never seen her get thrown.

"Sweetheart, you don't know God's plan. I have to believe, have to pray, that God's going to take care of you and this little one of yours."

Andie covered her face with her hands and Ryder couldn't stand still, couldn't let her hurt that way. There hadn't been a moment in their lives that they hadn't gone through the hard times together.

He wasn't going to let her go through this alone.

He didn't want to go through it alone.

In a few steps he was next to her. When he wrapped his arms around her, she buried her face in his shoulder and he held her close. Etta moved and he took her place on the bed, with Andie's arms around his waist. He leaned, resting his lips on the top of her head.

"I'm not going to let you down." He brushed blond hair back from her cheeks. "I won't let this baby down."

"I know you won't."

"Andie, the doctor wouldn't tell me anything. I really need to know what's going on." He brushed her cheek with a kiss and kept holding her.

She pulled back, nodding. "I know. I'll make sure she knows that you have to be included."

"Thank you." So, he felt a little better.

The curtain moved and Dr. Ashford walked in, clipboard in hand, glasses on her head. She smiled and pulled the glasses down, settling them on the bridge of her nose.

"Andie, I'm going to release you because there isn't a lot we can do but wait. I know that won't be easy, but that's what we have. The one thing you can do is take it easy and call me if you experience any bleeding." Dr Ashford stepped forward with a tube. "Here's the cream I told you about."

"Thank you, Dr. Ashford."

"Wait a second. I need more information. Isn't there anything we can do?" Ryder reached for Andie's hand and held it tight. Man, this wasn't the way it was supposed to go. He didn't want words like *time* and *waiting*.

"At this point there really isn't anything we can do. I'm sorry to be so blunt, but miscarriages happen in the first trimester. We don't always know why and we can't always keep it from happening. At this point the baby's heartbeat is steady and so we give Andie time. And she rests."

He met the doctor's gaze, and he was mad. She was a doctor. She was supposed to do something. That's why she was there, taking care of them. "She can stay in the hospital."

"Ryder." Andie squeezed his hand.

"Andie, we have to do more than wait."

The doctor put on a patient but slightly pained smile that didn't help him feel better, it just made him feel more out of control.

"If Andie was farther along and having contractions, we could put her in the hospital or give her medication to stop labor."

"So do that." Was that his voice, out of control, unreasonable? Dr. Ashford gave him another of her "poor man" smiles. He wasn't her first time at the circus; he was sure she'd met other clowns like him.

"This isn't a situation where medication will help. This is a situation for…"

"Prayer," Etta whispered.

The doctor nodded. "I would like for Andie to take it easy for a week or two, until the cramping stops. Let's see if we can get her through the third month, make it through the first trimester, and then we'll go from there."

Andie sniffled and her chin came up, because she wasn't giving up. He wanted to feel that strong right now, but instead, he felt like a kid who didn't have a clue.

The doctor kept talking, but when the words headed in the direction of female stuff, Ryder walked to the door. Or maybe hurried. These were words he could handle in connection to a cow or horse, but not to Andie.

He stopped at the curtain.

"I'll be waiting out here. When can she leave?"

"As soon as we get paperwork filled out. Straight home, straight to bed. She can get up to use the restroom and take showers. She can walk to the couch. But that's going to be it for now."

Ryder nodded and walked out. As he walked away he could still hear them talking, still discussing the best chance for the baby. He didn't want to hear about odds. He wanted to know that God was going to do something.

He hadn't expected that, to feel like this so soon, as if he'd push down a mountain to make sure his baby was safe. Baby. He remembered the ultrasound picture that showed something that looked like a tadpole. That was his kid in that picture.

He walked through the E.R., past other curtained cubicles, through doors that slid open as he approached, and then outside into cooler air and a light mist. He took off his hat and stood on the sidewalk with mist turning to rain. The sky was a heavy gray and the wind had died down.

For the first time he knew how it felt to need God so badly he'd bargain. He'd give himself for the life of his unborn child. He knew how it felt to be that man in Tim McGraw's song, begging God to take him, but not the girl, not the baby.

The door behind him opened. He glanced back and it was Etta. She smiled and walked over, looking up at the sky. "It's raining out here, Ryder."

"Yes, ma'am."

"You finding God out here?"

"Trying."

"He's as close as the words you're speaking. So

pray hard, boy. And then get that truck and drive it up to the building so we can take her home."

"I'll do that."

She touched his arm. "Ryder, this is going to work out."

He nodded and walked away. He hoped he wasn't going to let them all down. He didn't ever want a kid to feel the way he had. Let down.

When Andie got in his truck fifteen minutes later he was thinking about how he didn't want to let her down, either. He never wanted to find her alone, crying because he'd broken her heart.

Too many times in his life he'd seen his mom that way.

"You okay?" He shifted into gear and pulled away from the hospital.

"I'm not sure."

No, of course she wasn't. He wasn't sure, either.

Andie woke up late the following morning. She knew it was late because she could hear Etta downstairs washing dishes and the sun slashed a bright ray of light across her room. She'd made it through the night. It had been a long night. Ryder had refused to leave until about midnight. That's when Etta finally convinced him that his presence wasn't going to keep bad things from happening and they all needed some sleep.

She touched her belly, because her baby was in there, still safe, still a part of her world. "Stay in there, baby."

"Keep her safe." She looked up, knowing God heard. She tried to hold onto that faith, and not to fear. Every wrong thing she'd ever done flashed through her mind, taunting her as if her mistakes were a reason for God to take this baby, to make her pay. She pushed the thoughts from her mind.

Footsteps on the stairs signaled company. She waited and then there was a rap on her door.

"Come in."

"Are you decent?"

Ryder's voice. She looked down, at the sweats she'd slept in and the ragged T-shirt. "I guess so."

He pushed the door open and she brushed a hand through her hair, hoping to look less like something the cat coughed up and then trying to tell herself it didn't matter. It was just Ryder.

"I brought your breakfast."

He held a tray with a white foam container from the Mad Cow. He put the tray down, sitting it across her lap. She knew what was in the container. Pecan pancakes. And for the first time she knew she couldn't eat them. Her stomach turned and rolled, the way it had when she'd been ten and they'd gone to Branson for vacation. The more she thought of those curvy roads and the pecan pancakes…

"Move it, quick." Her stomach roiled and she dived as he reached for the trash can and stuck it under her face. If she breathed in, she'd lose it. If she closed her eyes and didn't breathe, that wouldn't be good, either.

"You okay?" He leaned down, a little green.

"Get rid of the pancakes."

"Got it." He grabbed the tray and as he headed out the door, she sat up. He peeked back inside the room. "Sorry about that."

"Not a problem," she groaned and leaned back on the pillows.

"I wanted to do something." He stepped back into the room, without the tray, and leaned against her dresser. He picked up a framed picture of the two of them on a pony she'd had years ago. His gaze came up, connecting with hers. "I feel like I need to take care of you."

"I don't want you to feel that way." She pulled her legs up and sat cross-legged on her bed. "This isn't us. We aren't uncomfortable, trying to figure out where we fit in each other's lives. I don't want you bringing me pancakes and holding the trash can for me. I don't want you to feel like you have to do this."

"But I do. You didn't get this way alone."

She stuck her fingers in her ears and shook her head, juvenile, but effective. "Don't."

He picked up the picture again. "It would have been easier to stay ten, wouldn't it?"

"Yeah, that'd be perfect. But it doesn't work that way."

"No, it doesn't."

"You don't have to stay here and take care of me. I know you have things to do, places to go."

"People to see?" He straightened and moved away from the dresser, a lanky cowboy with faded jeans and a hat that had been stepped on a few times. "I'm here, Andie. I'm in this for the long haul. This is the place where I'm supposed to be."

Etta popped into the room. "You're up. And you don't have to worry about a thing. Ryder fed the horses for you, and he even helped me pick the last of my green beans."

Andie swept her gaze from her aunt to Ryder. "You don't have to feed for me. You don't have to take care of me."

She didn't want to get used to him being there for her this way.

"Before you have this conversation, I wanted you to know that Caroline called. She asked about you and I told her what happened." Etta stood inside the door, not looking as apologetic as Andie would have liked.

"I wish you wouldn't have." The last thing she needed was for Caroline, her mother, to come rushing back to Dawson.

"She asked and I couldn't lie. And she said to tell you she loves you."

This couldn't be her life. Andie rubbed her hands over her face, trying hard to think about the mother who left, and the mother who had finally returned. Caroline had claimed she couldn't do it, couldn't be a mother to both of her daughters. At that moment it was harder than ever to understand how Caroline could walk away.

"It's okay, Gran." Andie smiled up at her grandmother. "Life changes, right?"

"It does change."

Etta slipped back out of the room. Andie could hear her careful steps going down the stairs. Ryder moved to the chair next to Andie's bed and sat down, taking off his hat and tossing it on the table next to him.

"You don't have to be here every day."

"You need to get over this." He raked his hand through his hair and let out a sigh. "I'm here because I want to be."

"You're here because you feel guilty, or obligated."

"No, I'm here because I'd be here no matter

what the situation. When have I not been there for you?"

She could have told him that he hadn't been there for her two months ago, when he hadn't answered her phone calls. But then she remembered last night and how he'd held her while she cried, how he'd been there for her when it really counted.

He had always been there for her.

"I know," she whispered. "But this isn't easy, not being able to get up."

"I have a feeling it'll only get worse."

"Thanks." She wiped at her eyes and ignored how he shifted in the chair and fiddled with his hat, not making eye contact.

"How do you feel today?" he finally asked.

"Cagey, kind of angry, and definitely tired of this bed."

He laughed. "You've only been there for about ten hours. Multiply a few times over and maybe you'll have an idea what the next couple of weeks are going to be like."

"Thanks for the optimism."

She leaned back in the bed and tried to push the days and hours from her mind. She could do this for her baby.

Ryder stood up, because he had a lot to get done, but first, he had to try one more time. He reached into his pocket and pulled out the ring that had been his grandmother's. He'd loved her, his grandmother. She had died when he was barely ten, but he remembered her smile, the way she'd listened when he told stories.

Andie focused on the pancakes that he'd set on the dresser. "I'll take those now."

"Okay." He reached for the foam container but he didn't hand it to her yet. She stared up at him, blue eyes rimmed with the dark remnants of mascara from the day before.

"Stop."

"What?" He stopped in the center of her bedroom, the room that hadn't ever changed. It still had framed photos of horses, a quilt made by her great grandmother and an antique rocking chair near the window.

Some things didn't change. And some did. No use looking in the rearview mirror when you're driving forward. An old rodeo friend had told him more than once. Greg was a rodeo clown and he raised race horses in Oklahoma City. He had a wife and kids, a real family.

People did manage to have families. He knew that. Men managed to stay married and stay faithful. Kids grew up with two parents in a home where they felt loved.

"Stop looking like that." Andie hugged her knees close to her body.

Ryder pulled the ring out of his pocket. He held it in one hand, the box of pancakes in the other and Andie's eyes widened as she watched him. She shook her head a little.

"Andie, please marry me. I haven't done the right thing very often in my life, but I really feel like this is the one time that I'm doing what needs to be done."

She actually laughed. "Seriously? That's your proposal."

He shoved the ring back into his pocket and handed her the pancakes. "What else am I supposed to say?"

"Love, Ryder. Marriage is about love and forever. Not 'doing what needs to be done.' Seriously, that's lame."

Well, thanks for that piece of information. He bristled because she was still smiling and he felt like a stinking fool.

"You'll have to forgive me if proposals aren't my strong suit. This isn't what I expected. I'm pretty sure it isn't what you expected. But we can sure do the right thing."

"I know we can, but this isn't it. I haven't put a lot of thought into marriage, either, but I can tell you one thing for certain, I'm not going to marry someone who doesn't love me."

"Love doesn't have too many guarantees, Andie. I know a lot of divorced couples who claimed to love one another. We've been through a lot together. We could make this work."

"And you'd end up resenting me. You might end up resenting the baby." She glanced up, her eyes were vivid blue and seeking something from him. He didn't have a clue what she wanted him to say.

She'd already pointed out that the proposal had been wrong. If that was the case, then he was pretty close to clueless.

"Fine, if the answer is no, then I'll live with it. But I'm this baby's father and I'm going to be here. I'm going to be a good dad."

"I know you will, Ryder."

Her eyes were soft and she already looked like someone's mom. And he still felt like the guy he'd been a month ago. Maybe she was right, he wasn't ready for this, for fatherhood.

Did other men just come equipped for this role?

"I have to go."

"Where…" She smiled. "I'm sorry, it isn't any of my business."

"I've got some bull calves that need to be taken care of. The vet's coming out this afternoon. Johnny Morgan is coming out to look at that mare I've been trying to sell."

"I wanted that mare."

"I thought you changed your mind."

She looked down and they were both thinking the same thing; he knew they were. She wouldn't be riding for a while.

Finally she smiled, "Yeah, I guess I've changed my mind. Johnny wants her for his daughter. I'm not sure that's a good match."

"I'll try to switch him to another horse then." He started to turn away, and he should have. Instead he leaned to kiss her cheek, just her cheek. "I'll be back later to check on you. Eat your breakfast."

She nodded and he walked to the door. His hand went to his pocket, to the ring that she'd rejected twice. She wanted to marry someone who loved her. He shook his head, not sure what to think about that.

If she didn't marry him, she'd marry someone else. Someday some other guy would know the right words. The thought turned around inside him. He didn't like to think of her married to another man. He tried not to picture it, her with another man's ring on her finger. His kid being raised by some other guy. What if that guy wasn't good to them? He thought if that happened, he'd have to hurt someone.

Or convince her to marry him before it happened. But the way things were going, he was far from convincing her that marriage was the right thing to do.

Chapter Ten

Andie woke up to the sound of footsteps coming down the hall toward her room. Lighter steps, not Ryder's. She blinked a few times and glanced at the clock. It was one o'clock. He'd left hours ago. A light rap on the door and then Alyson peeked in. Andie brushed her hair back from her face and sat up, already smiling.

"What are you doing here?" Andie hadn't seen her sister in weeks because of schedules and because she'd needed time to adjust to having this sister back in her life. Alyson had moved back to the area, but she'd had obligations, concerts she couldn't cancel.

Alyson shrugged, "I heard from a little birdie that you might need to be cheered up."

"You have a concert in L.A."

"Not until next week. And then I'm flying home to finish up the wedding plans. And you'd better get yourself together before the end of October so you can be my maid of honor." Alyson pushed the blankets aside and sat on the edge of the bed. "How are you?"

"Great."

"You're not great. If you were great you'd have something catty to say, or you might pick a fight with me. But you wouldn't have mascara smeared to your chin…"

"Seriously?" Andie rubbed at her cheeks.

"Seriously." Alyson walked to the dresser and picked up a small mirror. She pulled a few tissues out of the box. "You might want to get out of bed and wash your face, maybe brush your hair."

"I'm on bed rest."

"Yeah, but really, you can't go a month without brushing your hair."

Yes, she thought she could. If staying in bed was a way to hide from reality, she could do it. She took the mirror that Alyson held out to her.

Andie held the mirror up and ran her fingers through her hair, untangling it and then wiping away the mascara by method of the age old spit bath. "I look worse than something that cat of yours would drag in."

"Not even close." Alyson sat back down on the edge of the bed. "Do you want to talk?"

"About what? About making a huge mistake? About being pregnant? Or about the possibility that I could lose the baby?" Andie closed her eyes. "Do you know how guilty I feel? I told myself this baby is a mistake. I was upset about being pregnant. I resented what this would do to my life." She sighed. "If you notice, all three problems were about me, about how I would be affected. And now this is happening and the only thing I can think of now is how can I keep my baby safe."

"I think every single emotion you've had is probably realistic in your situation." Alyson pushed her over a little and scooted up next to her so that they were side by side on the bed, backs against the headboard.

Etta had told them they shared a crib when they were babies and when they moved to toddler beds they had refused to sleep alone.

And then they'd been ripped apart.

"I'm worried that I have too much of Caroline Anderson's DNA," Andie whispered. "What if I have a baby and then realize that I can't do this? What if I'm the type of mom who can't handle it?"

"You aren't our mother."

"I don't know that."

Alyson leaned close and their heads touched. "I do."

Andie nodded because she couldn't get the words out, couldn't tell her sister about Ryder's proposal, about him wanting to marry her, but not loving her.

"Let me help you with the wedding."

Alyson laughed. "You want to plan a wedding?"

"I can do something. I can at least keep you from making a frilly, lacy mistake."

"Okay, I'll get the books and you can help me. I need to pick out flowers. Oh, and your dress. I'm thinking pink."

"You're not."

Alyson laughed again. "No, I'm not. The wedding is going to be fall colors."

Andie sank back into her pillow as her sister left the room, her feet light on the stairs as she went down, calling for Etta. One sister happy, and one trying to be happy.

What if she said yes to Ryder? What would their wedding be like? Would it be a quick trip to a judge? Or something quiet on a weekday afternoon, just them, Etta and Pastor Jeffries.

As much as she'd never planned her wedding, Andie couldn't imagine either scenario. She groaned and covered her face with her hands. She suddenly wanted white lace and a man looking at her like she meant everything to him.

The way Jason looked at Alyson, not the cornered way Ryder looked at her. He hadn't ever looked at her this way, as if she was a stranger, or a problem he had to fix.

A cramp tightened around her stomach and she rested her hand there, praying the baby would stay safe, stay inside her where it could grow and be hers someday. Changes, life was definitely about changes.

She closed her eyes and thought about bargaining with God. But it wasn't about a bargain, it was about faith, about God's plan. She knew that and yet… She rested her hand on her stomach and fought against fear.

"You okay?"

Andie opened her eyes and smiled for her sister. "Yeah, I'm good."

"You don't look good."

"Pain. It isn't the same as yesterday. I think resting has helped. And the doctor prescribed some cream that is supposed to do something with my hormones."

"I'm glad." Alyson put down the pile of magazines. "You know I'll be here for you."

"I know you will." A year ago that wouldn't have been the case. But now, Alyson would be just down the road. Nothing ever stayed the same, Etta's song said. It was a bittersweet message of loss and gain.

"Ryder was down at the barn when I got here earlier."

"That's good." Andie wanted her sister to forget stories about Ryder. She pointed to the magazines as a direct hint.

"He's pretty sweet about all of this. When Etta mentions the baby, his eyes get damp. Cute."

"Right. Cute is what you want when coupled with, 'Hey, sweetie, let's get married. It's the right thing to do.' Isn't that cute?"

"What do you want him to say?"

Andie fiddled with the soft, worn edges of the quilt. Etta had threatened to get rid of it, but Andie loved it because it was familiar and comfortable.

"You want him to say that he loves you?" Alyson set books on the table next to Andie's bed. "Because you love him?"

"I don't really want to talk about it."

Alyson giggled and it wasn't like her, to giggle. Or to push. "So that's the way this is working out. You, the person who gave me advice to be careful with my heart, has lost yours."

"I haven't lost my heart."

But hadn't she? Wasn't it splintering off into tiny pieces, breaking apart each time he proposed with silly words about friendship and doing the right thing?

And as much as she didn't want her thoughts to turn that direction, she thought about what would happen to them if they lost the baby. What would happen if she said yes and then there wasn't a baby to hold them together?

The sight that met Ryder when he walked into his living room nearly undid him. He didn't need this after dealing with Andie and then working thirty head of rangy bull calves that weren't too partial to what the vet had to do with them. He stood in the doorway of his living room and stared. He counted to ten, reminding himself that they were little girls. But the little girls in question were sitting on his living room floor with sidewalk chalk, drawing pictures on his floor and his coffee table. He loved that table.

"What are you guys doing?" His voice roared a little, but he couldn't help it.

"We aren't boys." Molly stopped drawing long enough to inform him. "We're girls and we're drawing."

"That's sidewalk chalk." He scooped up the box and the chalk they weren't holding. "Sidewalk, as in outside, on concrete. Not inside on floors."

"We can wash it off." Molly kept doodling something that looked like a cat.

"Where's your dad?" Ryder held out his hand and they handed over the chalk they were still using.

Be a dad, he told himself. Be a dad. He knew

what his dad would have done if he'd caught Ryder and Wyatt doing something like this. It would have started with a belt and ended with the two of them not being able to sit down for a week.

That parenting example wasn't going to work so he had to think of something on his own. He looked down at the girls. They were staring up at him, two brown-eyed little angels with smudges of pink, green and yellow on their cheeks. Kat rubbed at her nose and left a dot of orange behind.

"I need for the two of you to come with me. We're going to clean this mess up and you're not going to do this again." Ryder motioned for the two girls to head for the door.

"What happened?" Wyatt asked, looking a little frazzled. His hair was too long and he hadn't shaved since he rolled into town with that moving truck.

How did a guy go from dating, rodeoing, living his own life, to this? He wasn't Mr. Family Guy. He didn't *do* baby wipes, diapers and cleaning up kid messes. At least that didn't used to be his life.

He sure wasn't going to raise his older brother on top of everything else.

Get used to it, big shot. His good self smirked at his bad self; as if there had been a major victory of some sort. Rip the good life right out from under a guy and then be happy about it.

"We're cleaning up a mess." Ryder answered and he glanced back over his shoulder, at what was obviously a zoo of chalk-drawn characters on his floor and table. "Where were you?"

Wyatt shrugged. "I had to figure out what to feed them for supper. I was in the basement going through the freezer."

"Yeah, well, feel free to go to the store."

"I'll do that." Wyatt took the chalk.

Ryder walked down the hall to the kitchen, his brother and nieces following. He dug through the cabinet under the sink and pulled out wipes that promised to clean kitchen cabinets, woodwork and bathrooms. All purpose, of course. He handed it to the girls.

"What do we do?" Molly stared at the container.

He smiled, because she was little and trying to act so big. And not once had she backed down when faced with his anger. He stayed on the floor, at eye level with her.

He wanted to hug her, not punish her.

"We're going to clean up the chalk. And I'll help you."

Molly's eyes lit up a little. "Okay."

He wasn't such a bad uncle. He stood up and

Molly took his hand. Kat grabbed his leg so he picked her up.

"How's Andie?" Wyatt followed him into the liv-ing room.

"I thought you were looking for something to cook?"

Wyatt took Kat from his arms. She had a wipe in her hands and she struggled to get down. Wyatt set her free to start cleaning. He stepped back, watching. Ryder lifted his gaze to meet his brother's.

"We'll just have Mad Cow again." Wyatt sat down next to Molly and showed her how to rub the chalk off the floor. "What about Andie?"

That was fine, Ryder didn't do family meals. He could slap some microwaved something on a plate, but the whole nutrition pyramid wasn't in his diet. He glanced back at the girls because they probably needed some of the stuff on that pyramid. At least Vera had vegetables at the Mad Cow.

Wyat cleared his throat, reminding Ryder of the question about Andie.

"She's doing good. I guess."

"You guess?"

"I proposed again. She turned me down again."

Wyatt moved from the floor to the sofa. "Well, how did you propose?"

"Are you the proposal expert?"

"No, but I've had more experience than you. At least with a real relationship."

"Yeah, well…"

"If you want her to say yes, you have to show her how special she is to you. You have to do more than pull out a ring and say, 'Hey baby, how 'bout we get hitched.'"

"Andie isn't about romance."

Wyatt laughed. "Have you been under a rock? She's a woman. She's having a baby, your baby. She wants romance."

"Chocolates and flowers?" Ryder hadn't ever bought a woman flowers.

"Do what you've always done. But maybe this time, mean it."

"She knows she's my best friend." Ryder showed Molly a spot on the floor that still had the smudged outline of a snake. She wiped it up with dimpled, pudgy hands. He looked at her hands and suddenly those hands meant everything. His baby would have hands like that, soft and pudgy. His kid.

But maybe his kid would have blond hair like Andie. Maybe she'd have his eyes, or his curls. He blinked and looked away from his niece, to the brother that was trying to give him advice.

"Ryder, I don't know how long you're going to

tell yourself that Andie is just a friend, but there's something you ought to think about."

"What's that?" He was still thinking about Molly's hands and he wondered how Wyatt felt the first time he held his daughter. But he didn't want to ask.

"You might ought to think about the fact that she's the longest relationship you've ever had."

His longest relationship. He brushed his hands down the legs of his jeans and smiled at Molly, whose wide eyes clued him in to the possibility that wiping dirt on clothes was bad.

"Yeah, I guess you're right, she is." He leaned and kissed Molly on the top of the head. She smiled up at him and then she went back to scrubbing.

"You think I might be right?" Wyatt got down on the floor to help his girls. "That's a huge change."

Ryder stood up, still holding the container of wipes. Yeah, huge change. But he'd had a lot of changes in his life. Not all bad. He watched the girls as they finished scrubbing his table. Change wasn't the worst thing in the world.

"I don't want to be like our dad. I don't want to mess up a kid the way we were messed up. Did you ever feel that way? Were you afraid to have kids?"

Wyatt looked at the girls. "Yeah, I was. I

learned something though. If you're worried about being like him, that means you know what he did wrong. You can make changes."

Ryder wondered about that. He wondered about Wyatt and the past year, trying to get his life back.

"Take my word for it, you can do this, Ryder. But first you have to make Andie feel like you love her, like she's your sweetheart, not the woman that lassoed you and dragged you down the aisle against your will."

Make her feel like his sweetheart? He had a feeling flowers and chocolate weren't the key to Andie's heart. And he had bigger problems than that. How did he go from thinking of her as his best friend to turning her into the person he loved?

He might not have all the answers, but he did know the way to her heart. And it wasn't chocolate.

It was dark outside when headlights flashed across the living room wall. Andie glanced out the window, but she couldn't see who it was. Alyson walked to the window and shrugged.

"I don't know who it is. It's a truck and a trailer." Alyson shot Andie a knowing look. "It's Ryder."

"Why can't he give me a break?"

"Because he's worried about you?" Alyson left the room and Andie knew she was letting Ryder in, and she imagined the two would share secretive little looks, maybe whisper something about her mood.

Staying down was not easy. She kicked her feet into the couch and screamed a silent scream of protest. When the footsteps headed her way she managed a calm smile.

"What are you doing here?" She flipped off the television when he walked into the room. He stood in the doorway, his hand behind his back. His jeans had pastel pink stains down the front.

Alyson peeked in, screwing up her face. "That's nice."

Andie drew in a deep breath and exhaled. "Fine, I can play this game. Ryder, it's nice to see you."

He smiled and stepped into the room, dark hair and dark eyes, and all cowboy. Except the pink stain. Her gaze kept straying to the pink blotch. But then his hands moved.

He had flowers and a sheepish grin as he held them out to her. She wanted to laugh. He actually had flowers. Her heart did something strange, because he'd never done that before. No one had ever bought her flowers. He hadn't even bought her flowers when he took her to the prom. Not even a wrist corsage.

"I wanted to check on you. I thought I'd see if there was anything you needed." He shrugged a little and he looked cute in jeans that had dirty smudges on the knees and a T-shirt that was a little threadbare. He didn't smell good.

"What have you been doing? You stink."

"Sorry, I worked with calves all day and then I had to go pick something up."

"You have pink on your jeans."

"Sidewalk chalk."

She pictured him on a sidewalk drawing hearts and flowers. He wouldn't have liked that image of himself.

He walked across the room with the flowers that were a little smushed and slightly wilted. She took them and held them to her nose. The rose in the bouquet flopped to the side with a broken stem. She peeked over the top of the flowers and smiled because his cheeks were ruddy from the sun and embarrassment.

"What did you have to pick up? The flowers?" She scooted up so he could sit on the couch next to her. He didn't sit down.

"No, I bought the flowers at…" He looked down, at boots covered in mud. On Etta's glossy wood floors. "I bought them at the convenience store."

They both laughed. At least they could still do that. "I love them."

"I bought you something else. I know you can't get up right now. But if you could sneak over to the window, I'll show you."

"Oh, okay."

And then he was gone. She waited a few seconds to see if he would come back. When he didn't she hurried over to the window and looked out. He was opening the back of the trailer. Her heart hammered a little harder than before.

It was dark but the light in the back yard glowed in the night and bugs buzzed around the front porch light. Andie leaned close to the screen and waited for Ryder to walk out the back of the trailer. When he did, she laughed.

He stopped in the yard, looking up at the window, at her. He motioned to the creature standing behind him. She pushed the window up.

"How do you like her?"

"A llama?"

"An alpaca." He sounded a little offended. "You said you wanted one."

"And I do. And she's beautiful. I love her."

"Etta can knit blankets with her wool."

"For the…" She bit down on her lip for a second. "For the baby."

He nodded and then he gathered up the lead rope of the animal. "Yes, for the baby. I'll put her in the corral with hay for tonight. Tomorrow we can see how she does with horses."

She watched until he was out of sight and then she hurried back to the couch. But Etta caught her. Etta, a dish towel in her hands and a frown on her face.

"What are you doing up?"

"Ryder had a surprise for me. I just slipped over to the window to see what it was."

"And it was what?"

She laughed. "An alpaca. Can you believe he got me an alpaca?"

"I think that's about the sweetest thing I've ever heard. Now, stay on that couch and I'll make hot cocoa."

An alpaca. Andie hugged her pillow and she couldn't stop smiling. The flowers were on the table, wilted but fragrant. And Ryder had bought her an alpaca.

She'd always known that sweet side of him. He'd always done the silliest things. The sweetest things.

And she'd never been able to think about falling in love with someone else, because she'd always loved him. She had dreamed of him someday loving her, someday asking her to marry him. But the dreams had been different.

The dreams hadn't included mistakes and this wall between them. The dreams had included words of love and forever, not the words *have to*.

She'd loved him forever and no one knew her secret but her. And probably God. The two of them knew how it had hurt to be his best friend while he dated, and never women like her. Ryder had dated women from Tulsa. He had dated the kind of woman she would never be, the manicured kind who always knew how to put outfits together, always looked stylish and beautiful.

His footsteps, minus boots, alerted her to his presence. She looked up as he walked through the door of the living room, without his hat, without boots. She smiled at his bare feet and he shifted a little, like he couldn't handle bare feet in her presence.

"Etta made me take my boots off."

"It's okay, you have cute feet."

He sat down on the coffee table facing her. "My feet aren't cute. I have long toes."

"My toes look like little clubs. Etta says because I went barefoot when I was a kid. I should have worn shoes." She stopped herself from rambling more. She looked up at him. "I love the alpaca."

"Nothing says I care like an alpaca." He winked and her stomach did this funny thing that felt like flips. How often had she watched him wink at girls, and then watched those same silly females follow him, not knowing that he wasn't good for much more than one date.

One night.

But they'd done everything together. They'd gone everywhere together. She'd been his comfort zone. He'd been safe with her. Maybe too safe, she decided.

"You're right about that." She couldn't look at him, her heart ached and it hurt to take a deep breath.

"Andie, I'm sorry. This isn't the way we planned our lives, but we can make it work. I'm going to be a good dad. I'll figure out how to be good at this."

"I know you will." She met his dark brown gaze and her heart thudded, her face warmed. "I know, because I know who you are, that you're good and kind."

"I'm not, Andie. I've never been good or kind. I've been shallow and selfish just about all of my life."

"Not to me."

He reached for her hand and she held her breath as he slid his fingers between hers. "No, not to you."

His eyes narrowed a little as he stared at their hands, and then he leaned. He leaned and he slid his free hand to the back of her neck, cupping it with a gentleness that made her heart melt. His lips touched hers, leaving behind the sweet taste of cola. Time slowed down and he held her close, keeping his lips close to hers. He moved, kissing her hair right above her ear and still holding her. He whispered but her brain didn't connect words that sounded as if he meant to hold her forever.

And then Etta cleared her throat. "Hot cocoa anyone?"

Ryder scrambled back away from her, leaving her alone and cold on the sofa. He stood up, looking sixteen and ashamed of being caught necking in the parlor. Andie smiled at this side of him, the soft and vulnerable side.

"I should go." He coughed a little. "I'll be back tomorrow. To check on the alpaca, and on you."

Andie nodded and then he was gone. From her seat on the sofa she watched his truck go down the road, back in the direction of his house.

He'd bought her an alpaca, and he'd kissed her goodbye. As much as she wanted to go back to being "just friends" she knew that could never happen.

Chapter Eleven

Ryder hadn't gone home the night before. Instead he'd left Andie's, driven past his house and straight to Tulsa. He hadn't been sure what he was going to do once he got there, but as he'd driven past a home store, it had hit him. He was going to have a kid, and that kid needed a room. A nursery.

Kids had rooms. Babies had nurseries. He'd learned a lot last night while he'd been shopping.

Two pots of coffee later, he stepped back and looked at the wall he'd been painting. It wasn't what he'd expected, but it wasn't bad. It was pretty good considering he didn't have a clue what he was doing. This was a far cry from painting a wall white, or beige.

"What are you doing?" Wyatt walked up beside

him. "I guess I know what you're doing, but isn't it a little early?"

"If a guy's going to have faith," the word wasn't easy to get out, "then he has to have faith. I'm going to be a dad and my kid is going to have the best nursery I can make."

"Green?"

"Yeah, green. For a boy or a girl." Ryder didn't look at his brother, he kept looking at the walls and he explained what the girl at the all night home store had told him. She'd said this was some shade of antique pastel green. And it would look great with cream trim on the woodwork. That's what the girl at the store had said.

He'd taken her word for it because he would have painted the room pink if it had been up to him. Pink because he couldn't stop thinking about having a little girl. As much as he'd ever wanted anything, the idea of that little girl in his arms had become the biggest dream ever.

Wyatt stepped over to the box Wyatt had placed on top of an old dresser. He started pulling out stuff that Ryder had bought on his late-night shopping trip. A train, a picture of a pony, a porcelain doll and a clown. Ryder still didn't like the clown. It looked too creepy for a baby's room. Wyatt shot him a look.

"That's the creepiest clown I've ever seen."

Wyatt dropped it back in the box. "So, trains, stuffed animals and butterflies?"

"It could be a boy or a girl. We won't know for a couple of months." We, as in he and Andie. He figured it would get easier to deal with, eventually.

But he thought most people planned these things and had time to adjust, to deal with it. He was going to be a dad and that hadn't been on any of his to-do lists.

He tried not to think of Andie losing the baby because he didn't really want to think about how that would make him feel. It didn't make sense that something he hadn't wanted, hadn't planned to have, could mean so much to a guy in a matter of weeks. It felt like something he wouldn't be able to handle losing.

His kid.

The whole nursery thing had happened after he'd kissed Andie earlier. Or had it been the night before. He glanced at his wrist, but his watch was on the counter downstairs. And none of that took his mind off that kiss. If a kiss, if holding a woman could make a man change his mind about having a woman in his life forever, that might have been the moment.

"What about a bed?" Wyatt finished rummaging through the box and looked at him.

"Our old cradle and crib are in the attic. I thought I'd sand them down."

"Wow, seriously?"

Anything for his kid.

"Yeah, a baby has to have a place to sleep."

Wyatt walked over to the rocking chair Ryder had bought last night. Every time he looked at that rocking chair he pictured it next to the window and he could see Andie in it, holding their baby. For that to happen, she'd have to marry him. She'd have to live here with him and make a home with him.

That didn't seem likely because she was pretty stuck on their "best friend" relationship. He had to take the blame for that.

"You're right—a baby has to have a place to sleep." Wyatt touched the rocking chair and his smile faded. Ryder thought Wyatt probably had images in his mind that were a little harder to face. Images of Wendy holding their girls.

Ryder slapped his brother on the back. "I think we need to go break a horse or something. All of this paint is starting to get to me."

"Wish I could, but the girls are waking up. I'm going to drive over to Grove. Do you need anything from town?"

"I was in Tulsa until three in the morning. What do you think?"

"Probably not. How did it go with Andie?"

"I bought her an alpaca."

Wyatt shook his head. "Okay, maybe you don't know what you're doing."

"What? She liked it."

"Yeah, she probably did."

Ryder grinned, "I bought her flowers, too."

Wyatt shook his head and walked out of the room. "You'll never get it."

Ryder dipped the brush in the paint and finished up a small section of wall that he didn't want to leave undone. Green, for a boy or a girl. The clerk at the home store had asked him all the details, like when was the baby due and did they have a name picked out. And he'd tried to think up answers because he didn't have any.

He tossed the brush into the tray and walked out of the room. A guy who was having a baby should have answers. By the time he pulled up to Etta's he'd managed to cool down.

Etta answered the door, motioning him into the kitchen and then looking at him like he'd dropped off the moon.

"Do you want a cup of coffee or a shower?" Her nose wrinkled and she stepped back. "Take your boots off."

"I guess I look pretty bad." He looked down. The pink chalk had faded but he had specks of paint on his shirt and arms.

"Not too bad. She's in the living room."

"Has she had breakfast? I could take her a tray."

"You might lose your head. She's already sick of staying down. She made Alyson drag that alpaca up to the window, right up on my front porch."

He laughed picturing that in his mind. Alyson was about the prissiest female he'd ever met. If she and Andie didn't look so much alike, he'd say there wasn't any way they could be twins.

"She'll be glad to see me." He took the cup of coffee from Etta. "Do you think she wants anything?"

"No, she can't have more coffee. One cup a day and she had eggs for breakfast."

He nodded and walked down the hall to the living room. He knew this house as well as he knew his own and as a kid he'd probably spent more time here than at home. He peeked around the door of the living room and Andie smiled. She didn't look mean. Or angry.

"Come in." She grimaced and looked him over, top to bottom. "You look horrible."

"Thanks." He sat down in the rocking chair, still holding his cup of coffee.

"You're wearing the same clothes you had on last night."

"Yeah, I am."

"And you haven't shaved."

He rubbed his hand across his cheek. It had been a couple of days since he'd shaved. "Andie, about the baby. What do you think we'll name her?"

She smiled and curled back into the couch. "Name her? I don't know. I mean, we don't know if…if she'll be a girl."

"But she might be."

"Yeah, she might be." Her eyes softened and she looked out the window. "I like the name Maggie."

"We could call her Magpie."

"Yeah, we could. And buy her a pony when she's three."

Andie looked at him and her smile faded. "Ryder, I don't want to do this."

"What, have the baby?" He could barely get the words out, but she was shaking her head.

"I don't want to plan. I don't want to think about names when I might lose her."

"That isn't going to happen." He wouldn't let it happen. The idea of this kid had settled inside him. The idea of Andie as the mother of his child was settling inside him, taking root. He tried to smile, for Andie's sake. "What happened to faith? What happened to trusting God?"

"I'm trying…I'm really trying, but I didn't expect this to be so hard." She bit down on her bottom lip and he'd never seen her like that—vulnerable. Her blue eyes were huge and her lips trembled.

Andie had always been the strongest woman he knew. She hadn't ever really seemed to need him, or anyone else. He always said she rolled with the punches.

But a baby changed everything.

He left the rocking chair and went to her side. She looked up, blue eyes swimming in tears that didn't fall. "I'll have enough faith for both of us. I can do that for you. I can do that for her."

And he meant it.

Step one in being a dad, trusting someone other than himself. Trusting God. He hoped God was still in the forgiving business because if Ryder was going to work on faith, he had a lot to confess to the Almighty. He had a lot of work to do on himself.

Andie leaned against a shoulder that was strong and wide and Ryder held her close. She sniffed into his shirt and pulled back.

"You really have to take a shower."

"Sorry, I should have done that before I came over, but I had to know. Last night someone asked me what we were going to name her, and when she'd be born, and I didn't know the answer."

"Where were you last night?" Ick, was that

jealousy? Andie shrugged it off. "I mean, you left here and..."

"I went to Tulsa to buy a few things for the house. And then I stayed up all night working."

She ran her hand down his arm, touching small spatters of green paint. She didn't want to take her hand off his arms. They were suntanned and strong. "Were you painting?"

"Yeah. You know, the girls are living at the house, and Wyatt."

"Oh." And it shouldn't have hurt. She should have been glad that he was doing something for the girls.

"Hey, let me get you some books. Or lunch. Would you like some chocolate?"

"Ryder, I don't need anything." She glanced out the window. "Except up from here."

"Yeah, I can't do that for you. What about Dusty?"

"I miss him. He probably thinks I've abandoned him." She wiped at her eyes. "Could you go out and check on him?"

"You know I will. But I wanted to check on you, first."

His voice was gentle but deep and he was still sitting on the coffee table, facing her. She brushed at her eyes again.

"Ryder, I'm so afraid."

"Why?"

She pulled back, looking at him, at a face she knew as well as she knew her own. She knew that dimple in his chin, the way his hair curled when it got a little too long, and the way his brown eyes danced when he was amused. And she thought he should know her, too.

"Because I don't know what's going to happen. I don't want to lose this baby. It was the most unexpected thing in the world, but now…" She wiped at her eyes. "She's a part of me. She's a part of us. As afraid as I am of raising her, I'm afraid of losing her."

"I'm not going to let you raise her alone." He grinned. "Or him."

That wasn't what she wanted him to say. She wanted him to say that he was afraid. But telling her she wouldn't be alone in this, maybe he was doing his best, the best a cowboy who had never planned on settling down could do.

It wasn't like he was going to suddenly pledge his undying love to her. She was lucky he'd agreed to go to church. He had promised to have enough faith for both of them. That was good, because her faith was pretty shaky at the moment and at least he was strong.

"I know you won't." She looked out the window. A car drove down the road, a rare thing for their street at this time of day. It didn't stop.

It went on down the road, the distraction ended.

And her heart was still aching because she was going to have a baby and she wanted more than anything to hear Ryder say he loved her.

"You should go. I know you have a lot to do today." She didn't want him to feel like he had to stay and take care of her.

She wanted to get up and take care of herself. She'd thought about it earlier, before anyone was up. She'd considered sneaking out of the house and going outside to check on her horse and see the alpaca. And small twinges of pain had convinced her otherwise.

As hard as it was to stay in bed, she didn't want to take chances.

"I don't have a lot to do, Andie. I've been getting things taken care of. Today I'm here to take care of you."

She squirmed a little. "I really don't think that's a good idea."

"Why?"

"Because that isn't us."

"It's the new us." He sniffed his own shirt. "But I do need a shower."

"Ryder, really, you don't have to stay here and take care of me. I have Etta and Alyson. They'll take care of me."

Ryder stood up. "This isn't just about you, Andie, this is about our baby. I'm taking care of you and our baby."

"I don't need to be taken care of."

"Of course you don't, you stubborn female." He walked to the door. "I'll be back in an hour."

The front door slammed and then she heard him backing out of the driveway and then shifting as he headed back down the road. She picked up one of the wedding magazines that Alyson had been looking at.

White and frilly. Couldn't a wedding be practical? She was practical. She wouldn't want a dress she couldn't wear again. She wouldn't want cake that looked beautiful but tasted like dust.

If she was to get married she'd want daisies and denim. She'd want to ride off into the sunset on her horse and camp in the mountains for her honeymoon. With her baby next to her. But who was the groom in this little dream? The guy who wanted to take care of her?

Her hand went to her belly and she whispered, wondering if it was true that babies could hear from inside the womb. But a baby the size of a shrimp? She really didn't like that image.

She preferred picturing the full-sized baby, with brown hair and brown eyes. Her imagination fast-forwarded her ten years and she was still living with Etta, raising her daughter. But in the dream, Ryder was a visitor and a woman waited in his truck as he picked up his daughter for the weekend.

That wouldn't do. But neither did the other version of the dream, the one where she and Ryder were together but he resented her, resented their child because the ring on his finger kept him tied to them.

As she drifted on the edge of sleep she told herself that wasn't fair. It wasn't fair to Ryder that she was putting him in the role of villain. Ryder had always been honorable. He had always been there for her.

But having a baby, neither of them knew how to approach this mountain. She had made mistakes in her life, mistakes that she knew God had gotten her through, helped her to overcome. As she laid there she thought about her baby and she couldn't call a child a mistake.

The baby was a choice they had made. It might not have been the right choice, but it was one they would work through. And it would never be the baby's fault. She would never let that happen.

A truck door slammed and she jumped but then settled back onto the couch. She listened to boots on the wood front steps, a rap on the door and then Ryder walked into the living room. He had shaved and his hair was damp and curled a little.

"Wake up, sweetheart, you're going outside."

"What?" She sat up, but she didn't reach for the flip flops on the floor next to the sofa.

"I'm going to work Dusty, but I thought you'd like to go. You can sit on a lawn chair out there."

"You think that would be okay?" She reached for her shoes.

"Don't stand up."

"What?" She held her shoes and then he was standing in front of her, leaning to pick her up.

"I'm going to carry you." He scooped her up and she grabbed quick, wrapping her arms around his neck.

"I'm too heavy."

"You're not heavy." He laughed and jostled her, shifting her. "No, you're not heavy. I've picked up bales of hay that weigh more."

"Thanks, I'm a bale of hay." She leaned and he did smell better. Soap, aftershave and the minty smell of toothpaste. He turned a little and they were face-to-face, practically nose to nose.

"You're not hay," he whispered. He touched his forehead to hers and then looked away, his arms tensing, holding her close.

What was she to him? Okay, she got it, she wasn't hay. But if she asked, what would he say? Best friend, pain in the neck, or was she now just extra baggage that he wasn't sure how to handle?

Andie wasn't heavy. She held him tight, her arms around his neck, and her head close to his.

He carried her down the hall and into the kitchen. Etta was sitting at the table with a basket of yarn, knitting needles in her hand and something partially made. She looked up as they walked into the room.

She set the knitting needles and yarn on the table and stared for a moment before shaking her head. "What do you think you're up to?"

"Going outside." He stopped at the screen door and waited for Etta to tell him he was crazy and why he shouldn't do this. But the more he thought about Andie stuck in the house, the more he knew he had to get her outside.

"She has to stay down," Etta warned.

"I'm not going to let her walk, just letting her get fresh air. We can't keep her locked in the house for nine months."

Andie moved in his arms. "I don't think I'll be on bed rest for seven months."

"Well, probably not, I'm just saying that you could use some fresh air."

Etta shook her head again. "I think the two of you were meant for each other."

Meant for each other.

Ryder couldn't respond to that. He pushed the screen door open with his hip and slid through. Andie pushed to keep the door from hitting them on their way out. She was easy in his arms, and he'd never thought of the two of them as a couple. As "meant for each other."

Or maybe he had. Maybe he'd pushed it from his mind because it was easy to be her friend and the idea of breaking her heart had been the thing that scared him the most. He'd never let himself think about the two of them together. She had always been his best friend.

He'd picked safe.

"What?" She quizzed as he sat her down in the lawn chair, cradling her close as he settled her in the seat.

"Nothing."

"Whatever. I think I've known you long enough to know when nothing is really something. You're jaw is clenching because you're grinding your teeth. You do that when you're mad about something."

"I'm not mad."

"Are too."

"Not right now, Andie. I can't have this conversation with you right now."

"Yeah, I guess we're talked out."

No, he thought they probably had plenty to talk about, just nothing they wanted to talk about. "When's your next doctor's appointment?"

"Next week." Her hand went to her belly and she looked away from him.

"Are you," he squatted next to her, "are you having pains?"

She drew in a deep breath. "Some twinges, but nothing too bad. Sometimes I'm afraid…"

He'd never heard her admit that before. "I know, me, too. But I'm praying."

"You're praying?"

"Every time I take a breath." He couldn't stop looking at her belly, because his baby was in there. He'd never thought it could change him like this, that child and Andie needing him.

"One of us has to be strong, Ryder."

"You can count on me." He stood and she was staring up at him. "What do you need me to do with Dusty?"

He backed away, hoping she'd let the conversation end.

"I think lunge him in the arena. He doesn't like it when you ride him." She pulled her sweater closer around herself.

"Yeah, I seem to remember the last time I rode him. I think I still have the scar on my arm where he dumped me."

She smiled at that and picked up the cat that had left the barn and was circling her chair. When her smile faded and her eyes clouded over, he knew he should have left when he had the chance.

"Ryder, what if I lose the baby?"

How was he supposed to answer that? Two months ago having a baby was the farthest thing from his mind. And now she wanted to know what they'd do if she lost it? Having that baby meant changing his life in ways he hadn't planned.

Now, not having it felt like the change he didn't want to face.

"We're not going to lose the baby." He bent and kissed the top of her head. "I'm going to catch Dusty."

She might have whispered "chicken" as he walked off. He couldn't be sure of that, and he wasn't positive it wasn't just his own thoughts calling him names.

But yeah, he was a chicken. That was something he was just now figuring out about himself. He was a big old chicken. He was afraid of conversations with obstetricians. He was afraid to talk about having kids with Andie.

He was not afraid of a horse. He whistled and Dusty didn't even lift his head. That horse was not going to make him walk out into the field and catch him.

Chapter Twelve

The house was quiet. Andie hated the quiet. She hated being inside. She hadn't been out since the day Ryder had carried her outside to watch while he worked Dusty. He'd meant it to be a good thing, but instead it had ached inside her, watching him work her horse.

At least she'd gotten to go out.

Since then it had been daily visits. He showed up with food from the Mad Cow or movies for her to watch. He'd sat with her while she dozed. He constantly asked how she was and if she needed anything. Her heart was getting way to used to him being around.

Today it was raining, a cold rain that blew leaves against the windows while thunder rumbled in the clouds. And everyone was gone. Alyson was in Tulsa with Etta, getting the finishing touches on her dress. Ryder was selling off a herd of year-old steers. She'd promised she would stay on the couch. She had food. She had a thermos of cold water.

She had cabin fever like nobody's business.

Somewhere in the distance a dog barked, the sound getting swallowed up by thunder and rain beating on the roof of the porch. Andie strained to listen. She heard it again and then a cow.

Normal farm sounds, she told herself. Dogs barked and cows mooed. The only thing that wasn't normal was her, and the fact that she couldn't go check and see what was going on.

The barking got louder, more frantic.

"Okay, I can't sit here." Andie picked up her cell phone and slipped her feet in tennis shoes by the door. She grabbed a jacket off the hook on the wall and walked outside. For a moment she stood on the front porch, protected from the rain. Of course the dog stopped barking when she walked outside.

Andie walked off the porch and headed across the yard, in the direction of the most pitiful mooing she'd ever heard. Her stomach twisted, because she didn't know what she'd find, and because she shouldn't be up.

But she hadn't had pains for two days. That had to be a sign that things were getting better. She was close to finishing her first trimester.

She scanned the fence, looking for the cow and

the dog. They were quiet for a minute and then it started again. The dog barked an excited bark, not angry. Picking up her pace she headed for the clump of brush and stand of trees near the corner of the fence. The dog barked again. And then she saw the cow on the ground. It bellowed, low and pitiful, sides heaving. The dog was crouched on the ground, tail wagging. It turned to look at her, tongue hanging out. It didn't leave the cow.

Now what?

Andie slid between two rows of barbed wire and approached the cow, talking quietly to calm the poor heifer. "I know, it's scary, isn't it? Poor thing, you don't know what's happening to you."

The cow looked up, her eyes huge, her mouth opening in a pant that became a low moo. Andie squatted next to her, running her hands over the animal's heaving sides. Cows never picked good weather or good conditions to calve. And if they were going to have problems, which they often did, it always happened at the worst possible time.

Andie had pulled a calf two hours before her senior graduation. That's how life worked on the farm. She'd pulled a calf, and then she graduated from high school.

But this was different. A cow in distress, but

Andie's baby, needing a chance, needing to be safe.

One hoof was out. Andie couldn't begin to guess how long the cow had been down or how long she'd been trying to push this baby out.

It was her first calf and she was obviously going to be like her mother, having difficult deliveries. But Andie couldn't help her. Any other time, but not today. It wasn't a difficult decision to make. It really felt like the only decision.

Etta had ordered her to call Ryder if anything happened, or if she needed anything. He had his cell phone on and was just minutes away. This qualified as an emergency, as needing something. She let out a sigh, because she hated having to call him away from what he was doing. To take care of what she needed to have done.

But this wasn't about her. It was about the baby.

She stood up.

The dog, a stray that had showed up in town a year or so ago hurried to her side, wagging his entire back end. He hadn't run the cow, she was sure of that. He'd just been sending out his own alert. He sat down next to her, proud that he'd done his job.

Andie pulled out her cell phone and dialed. Ryder answered after a few rings.

"Andie?"

"Ryder, I have a cow in labor. I think the calf is going to have to be pulled."

"Are you outside?"

"Yes, I'm outside." She wiped rain from her face but it kept coming down, soaking her hair and clothes. "I had to see what was going on."

A long pause and then he spoke. "Andie, get back inside."

She could hear sounds in the background. Laughter, conversations and dishes rattling. It riled her that he was ordering her back into the house. When had he ever done that?

"I can't leave the cow."

"You have to leave her." His voice got loud, firm. "I'll be there in five minutes."

"Fine." She slid the phone back into her. "Help is on the way, girl."

The cow mooed and raised her head. "You're right, I'm not going to leave you alone."

No one wanted to be alone in a situation like this.

Andie backed up to a tree that was just a few feet away. It gave her a little protection from the rain, a little shelter. But the whole time she stood there, waiting, she felt mad and guilty. She didn't want to feel, either.

Ryder grabbed the ticket for his lunch at the Mad Cow and reached into his pocket for his wallet. He was trying to look casual, as if this was something he did every day, getting calls from Andie and leaving in the middle of lunch.

But lately, nothing was what he'd been used to doing every day. He looked at the guys he'd had lunch with—Clint Cameron, Adam Mackenzie, Reese Cooper and a couple of others. They were all taking their lunch break at the Mad Cow. A few of them were getting ready to go to the live-stock auction. Reese was getting ready for the rodeo finals in Vegas. They were all still living the lives they were comfortable with.

Without warning, Ryder's life had become something so upside down he didn't recognize it. Church yesterday with Wyatt and the girls and afterward he'd taken lunch to Andie. A couple of weeks ago he'd found out he was going to be a dad. And each and every day he was climbing up the biggest mountain of his life, trying to find his way back to God and his way forward in this situation with Andie.

For a while it had been like wearing someone else's boots. But he was adjusting. And everyone at the table was looking at him like they thought maybe he was going to lose it if they didn't hitch him to an anchor.

Clint reached for the ticket Ryder was still holding.

"You go on, that sounded like something that needs to be taken care of. I'll buy your lunch."

"Andie has a cow down." He picked up his burger to take it with him.

"Do you think you'll need some help?" Adam MacKenzie grabbed the ticket from Clint and pulled out his wallet. "I'll get lunch."

Clint laughed. "Will he need help with what, Andie or the cow?"

Ryder threw money on the table for the tip. "You guys are hilarious. I don't think I'll need help with either."

Reese, chair tilted back on two legs, was grinning. And Ryder kind of wanted to hit him, because Reese had dated Andie back in their college days. He'd dated her and cheated on her. It had mattered then, it mattered more now.

"I never thought you'd be the guy falling like this." Reese finally commented. Clint jerked his chair back and Reese scurried to get his feet back under him as the chair went to the floor with a crash that had people staring and Vera running from the back.

The owner of the Mad Cow glared at them and then she headed toward Ryder with foam containers. "Are you heading out?"

"Yeah, Andie called." He shot Reese a look. "She has a cow down. I need to run but Adam's buying lunch."

"I wasn't worried about you skipping out on a bill, Ryder. I was worried about Andie. I saw you here and I know Etta's in Tulsa, so I made Andie up some of my special cashewed chicken. Take this to her. And let me have that." She grabbed a napkin out of the holder on the table and reached for the burger he was about to take a bite of. Before he could object she opened the Styrofoam and put the burger inside. "There, now you're all set to go. And you'd better hurry or she'll be hooking up a pulley to her truck and pulling that calf on her own."

"I know." He kissed Vera on the cheek. "You're the best.

He pulled into Andie's a few minutes later. She was sitting on the porch, out of the rain. She didn't stand up when he pulled up to the house. Worry knotted in his stomach. He should have ignored her when she said she didn't need him here. He could have found someone to do his work at home and he could have sat with her while Etta was gone.

He jumped out of the truck, grabbing the container of food before he shut the door. Andie crossed her arms over her front and glared as he hurried toward her. She was mad. He guessed that was a plus.

"What took you so long?"

"Had to get our food." He felt the need to

defend himself. "And it didn't take that long. Here's your lunch. Vera made you some of her cashewed chicken."

She took the container from him. "The cow is over there, near the corner post and that clump of brush."

"She'll be fine, Andie. Why don't you go inside?"

"I couldn't sit in there. I'll sit on the porch. This isn't walking around. This isn't doing something." Her hands clenched into the sleeves of her sweater.

"I know." He took a few steps back to keep from holding her when he knew being held was the last thing she wanted. He knew her, knew she was close to tears that she was fighting hard against. There were times to hold a woman and let her cry. He knew this wasn't one of those times.

"I'm so tired of this." She brushed her hands over her face and didn't look at him. "I'm so tired of not being able to take care of things. And having to call someone to take care of things I can usually take care of. And then there's the guilt because I got up to see what was wrong."

"It's okay to be sick of this, you know."

"But the baby…" she began.

"Is going to be fine. You're going to be fine."

"You don't know that," she insisted.

Now was when a man held a woman and let her cry. He sat down next to her on the wicker bench that always creaked with his weight and she leaned into his side. He heard the cow mooing and tried to ignore it.

"Andie, we're almost to the three month mark. What have we got, another week or two?"

"Yeah."

"So, we're going to make it." He held her and felt her tense and pull away.

"You have to go deliver that calf. I can't lose that calf."

"I'm going."

He hurried out to his truck and found rope, a coat and some old towels. He kept the metal toolbox on the back of his truck stocked with just about everything he might need in an emergency. As he dug around inside the box he found a rain poncho that he'd never taken out of the package. Now that was prepared.

The dog greeted him as he walked across the yard. The scruffy looking terrier cross was mud-caked but happy. He'd never seen a dog like this one, one that always looked as if it was grinning. He guessed if everyone in town was feeding him, he'd be pretty happy, too.

The cow was still laboring. He climbed the fence and eased toward her. The wild look in her eyes warned that she wasn't going to be pleasant about dealing with him. Good thing she was nearly worn out. That was a bad thing, too. It meant she wasn't going to be a lot of help pushing this calf out.

"How is she?" Andie had moved to another seat on the porch and she leaned out. He knew it was killing her, this inactivity, and not taking care of her farm.

"She's having a baby, Andie. Now give me a minute." He looped the rope around the tiny hooves that were trying to poke out.

It wasn't the worst case he'd ever seen. It wasn't going to be the easiest. He probably should have taken Adam up on his offer to help.

"Do you want me to call for help?" Andie asked.

He shook his head and she'd have to deal with that answer for now. The cow tried to get to her feet but couldn't. Oh man, that wasn't what he needed. He turned back to Andie and she was still leaning out, still watching.

"Call Clint."

He got the calf delivered before Clint got there, but the cow was still down. "Momma cow, we need you to get up and take care of this baby."

It happened sometimes, a cow got down, got sick and that was just the end of it. He couldn't look at Andie, sitting on the porch. He knew she'd be out there fighting to save that heifer if she knew what he suspected.

Clint's truck pulled into the driveway and Adam was right behind him. Ryder had never had a sentimental day in his life, but right at that moment, it was a pretty good feeling to be from his hometown. It was good to be where people knew him and where he didn't have to go far to find a helping hand.

The two were armed with calf starter in a bottle for the calf, several bottles of medication and a needle to give the cow the necessary shots. They climbed the fence as Ryder dried off the calf. It was the most pitiful looking little black baldy calf he'd ever seen. Black with a white face, its sides were caved in from dehydration and it kept coughing from the gunk in his lungs.

"That's a shame." Clint had lowered himself next to the cow and he injected her with antibiotics. "She's a good little heifer."

"Yeah, and if we don't do something, Andie's going to be down here trying to get her on her feet." Ryder took the bottle that Adam carried and pushed it into the little calf's mouth. It moved away a few times and then finally started to suck. It didn't take long for the little guy to put down the two liters of milk.

"Let's see if we can get her on her feet." Adam grabbed the rope that Ryder had used to pull the calf. It was soaked and muddy. "What do you think?"

Ryder shrugged, so did Clint. Clint took the rope and put it around the cow's neck. Ryder was dealing with a calf that now thought he must be mommy. It was sucking at his jeans and at the hem of this T-shirt. It would have been cute if buckets of rain hadn't been falling on them and the momma cow hadn't been on her side in a puddle of water.

They were heaving on the cow when Andie came traipsing across the yard again.

"What are you doing up?" Ryder was in the process of sliding a rope under the cow's middle.

She stopped at the fence and watched. "I had to check on her because I know you aren't going to tell me everything."

"Andie, you have to get back on the porch. If Etta comes home and you're standing down here in the rain…" He stopped. "You know, it doesn't matter what Etta is going to say. You're an adult and you know better."

"Tell me how she is."

"She's going to die if we don't get her up."

"Ryder." Clint's voice was a little softer and Ryder thought that had to be Willow's influence. When had Clint Cameron ever been the guy with the soft touch. "Andie, we'll get her up and if we can get her in the trailer on my truck, I'll take her home and work with her. We'll get her back on her feet. You might have to bottle feed that calf, though."

"Thanks, Clint." Andie shot Ryder a smug smile. "Now I'll go sit back down. Just consider this my shower for the day."

Ryder watched her go. Rain was pouring down, and a crack of thunder gave him the motivation he needed to kick it up a notch. He had no desire to be standing under this tree when lightning hit.

Clint pulled on the rope, heaving and out of breath and Adam helped Ryder push the back end of the cow as she fought to get up.

She was finally on her feet.

"Let's take her out this corner gate right to the trailer." Clint leaned to catch his breath.

"We can take her to my place." Ryder didn't have his trailer, but they could put her in Andie's.

"Ryder, you have enough going on right now with Wyatt at your house and Andie needing you here. Let us do this one for you."

"I can manage."

"I didn't say you couldn't." Clint pounded him on the back. "But I'd say you've got your plate pretty full right now. And the next few months aren't going to get any easier."

"That's great to know."

Clint laughed, but he was still working, still moving the cow and working with her. "Yeah, well, that's how life is. When you think you've got it all figured out and think you know your next move, God surprises you with something huge. But seriously, it's about time you and Andie realized what the rest of us have known forever."

"Known?" He'd never _had_ such a hard time forming sentences.

"Yeah, known." Clint shot him a look like he really should be getting it. "You and Andie haven't been far from each other's side in years. And when you thought Reese hurt her, you broke his nose."

"He deserved that."

"Yeah, he probably did." Clint led the cow a few wobbly steps toward the gate that Adam had opened. "But most guys wouldn't bust their buddy's nose for just any girl."

"She's..." He wasn't going to get baited into this conversation. Clint and Adam shot one another knowing looks and Ryder decided to ignore them. The odds of him taking the two of them were pretty slim, so it made sense to load the cow and forget this conversation.

He walked away from Clint's trailer telling himself that this was just part of his new life. Every guy in town was dating, getting married or recently married. And they didn't want to suffer alone.

Andie reheated Ryder's cheeseburger up while he changed out of his T-shirt into a button up shirt he found behind the seat of his truck. When she heard him coming down the hall she poured a cup of coffee and sat it next to the plate.

Domestic. She'd never been one of those females, the kind that loved to cook and clean. She could make a decent burger or pancakes, she could brew pretty terrific coffee, but she had never seen herself as June Cleaver or Martha Stewart.

Ryder walked into the kitchen, stopping at the door. He eyed her, eyes on the meal and the coffee, and then back to her. She ignored him and poured herself a glass of milk, because she'd had her cup of coffee already.

"You should be sitting down. I could have done this. I could have made coffee." He didn't sit down.

"I wanted to do something for you. You've been doing everything for me for the past couple of weeks."

"That's because you've needed me to be that person, Andie. There's been plenty of times you've taken care of me."

"Yeah, but this is just not right, all of this sitting and letting people wait on me."

"You're not doing it because you're lazy. You're taking care of our baby. And I'm taking care of you." He pointed to the hall and she knew what that meant. "Back to the parlor, sweetie."

She grabbed her milk and walked past him down the hall. He followed a few minutes later with his coffee and plate of food. When he walked through the door she was back on the couch, her feet up, the pillow over her face.

He had the nerve to laugh.

She tossed the pillow at the end of the sofa. "You think this is funny?"

"I think you're suddenly a drama queen and you're not very good at it."

"How's my cow?"

"Clint thinks he can save her. You know how it is, Andie. She's in bad shape. The calf drank, though. We got some colostrum for him and added it to the milk replacer in the bottle."

"Thank you." She hugged a pillow to her stomach. "I'm sorry I had to call you."

"I'm not." He finished his burger and set the plate down. "Now, tell me what I can get you? Chocolate? Books? Something to drink?"

"Nothing." She pointed to the obvious. "I have books. I have magazines. I have the TV remote. The only thing I don't have is my life. I shouldn't resent that, should I?"

"I think it's probably natural."

"I don't want this baby to feel resented. What if she can feel it now, that I'm sick of sitting. I don't blame her, though. This is my fault. This whole pregnancy is my fault. You didn't ask for this to happen to you. If it wasn't for me, you'd be on your way to Vegas to the finals."

"Andie, I'm not blaming you. And this pregnancy isn't your fault. We, I think that's how this works. I made a decision to stay here. This is where I need to be. The finals aren't that important."

"Right. And you'll never resent that a night with me changed your life? This is exactly what we were worried would happen. We can't go back to being friends. I'm not even sure if we can go back to being us."

He moved to the table, the place that had become his in the past couple of weeks. She met his gaze, the dark eyes that always looked at her as if he knew her better than anyone else knew her.

"Andie, we'll make this work. We'll deal with it."

"Right, that's what we'll do, deal with it." She leaned back away from him, against the cushioned arm of the sofa and she closed her eyes. "I need to take a nap. That's one of the symptoms of the first trimester of pregnancy, being tired."

"I'm not leaving."

He got up and moved to the cushioned rocking chair a short distance away. He looked out of place in Etta's parlor and in that prissy chair. She smiled, watching him try to get comfortable. He stretched jean-clad legs in front of him and crossed his legs at the ankles. His hat was low over his eyes and he crossed his arms in front of him.

She was the one needing a nap and he'd probably be asleep long before her. If she even fell asleep. Mostly she wanted an excuse to stop talking about their lives and how everything had changed.

One thing hadn't changed. She loved Ryder. But Ryder thought she was nothing more than his best friend.

And the mother of his baby.

Chapter Thirteen

Something woke Andie up. A bad dream? A bad feeling. She turned and she was on the edge of the sofa. She moved back to keep from falling off. It took her a minute to put it all together, to remember that it was Tuesday and Etta was in Tulsa with Alyson. She sought the person who had been there with her when she fell asleep.

Ryder was still in the rocking chair. His head was bent forward, his hat covering his face. Soft snores drifted across the room. She smiled and curled back into the blanket that hadn't been on her when she fell asleep. And she tried not to think about it, about him hovering over her, covering her with the afghan that had been folded at the other end of the sofa.

Pain slid through her abdomen, catching her by surprise, taking her breath.

That's what had awoken her. It hadn't been

a dream. It hadn't been just a bad feeling. She rubbed her belly and waited for it to end. It didn't. The cramping wrapped around her lower abdomen and held on.

"No," she whispered but it woke Ryder.

"What?" His voice was groggy his eyes a little foggy from sleep.

She needed a minute, just a minute to get her thoughts straight.

"I'm cramping again." She met his gaze and his brow furrowed. "It's my fault for going out to check on the cow."

"We left you here alone. I should have stayed with you." He stood. "We aren't going to sit and talk about this being someone's fault. We don't know what this is, or even if there's something that could be done to stop it."

"I know." Her heart tightened with dread, because she knew that there was nothing a doctor could do, not at this stage in her pregnancy.

He grabbed her shoes and a jacket that she'd left on the other chair. "Come on, let's go."

"Go?"

"To the E.R. Andie, we're not going to sit here and do nothing. We'll call Etta on our way."

"I don't want to call Etta. Alyson deserves to have this day without me interfering."

"Alyson would want you to interfere if…"

If she lost the baby. Andie slid her feet into the

shoes he set on the floor for her and then she let him hold the sweater for her to slide her arms into the sleeves. They felt like a couple. She closed her eyes against another sharp wave of pain, and a similar one that invaded her heart that asked her what became of them tomorrow.

"I don't want to lose my baby." She looked up at him, not wanting to need him, but she did.

He sat down on the sofa with her. He touched her cheek and turned her to face him. "I know."

His kiss was sweet, gentle, and it made her feel strong. It made her feel loved. And she knew that wasn't what he meant to do with that kiss. She sighed into his shoulder and he hugged her close.

"Let's go, Andie."

She walked out the door at his side, her hand on her belly, her baby still safe inside her. And thoughts invaded, because she knew that when she returned to this house, everything might be different. The last thing she saw was the pile of clothes on the table next to the door, the little baby clothes that Etta had found in the attic, and an afghan that Andie's mom had tried to crochet years ago—when Andie was a baby.

The E.R. was bustling with late afternoon activity. Rush hour in Grove always resulted in plenty of minor fend-benders the nurse informed them as they got Andie settled in a bed.

"You can't leave me this time." Andie waited until the nurse left and then she grabbed Ryder's hands. "Don't leave me."

"I'm not going anywhere."

"Please, don't be angry with me."

He sat down on the edge of the bed. "I'm not angry, Andie, I'm worried. This is my baby, too."

"I know."

"Do you? Because sometimes you act like you're in this alone. And you're not. We were both surprised by this, but I'm no less invested in this pregnancy than you are." His voice cracked. "That's my kid. It isn't something I planned, but after a couple of weeks, a guy starts to get used to the idea."

"I'm so afraid that this is God's way of punishing me."

He rubbed his thumb over her fingers. "Andie, you thought being pregnant was punishment. Now you think God's punishing you with problems. Why? Do you think God is sitting up there waiting for you and you alone to mess up so He can come up with new ways to punish you?"

"Consequences?"

"Yeah, okay, consequences. But you're wrong about this." He leaned close, touching her cheek. "Your whole life you've worried about being good enough. That's your mom's fault. And your fault for blaming yourself for her skipping out on you."

"If I'd been easier…" She choked on sobs that came in waves and Ryder grabbed her up and held her close.

"She messed up, not you."

"How does a mom walk out on a kid?" She leaned into his shoulder and all of the pain of her childhood came out, all of the feelings of being defective. Ryder held her tight, rubbing her back.

"You're not your mom."

"No, I'm not." She wiped at her eyes and moved away from him. "But if I lose the baby, you're off the hook."

"Oh, so now I'm your mom?"

"I don't know, Ryder. I don't even know what I'm feeling right now." More tears rolled down her cheeks and this time Ryder didn't hold her. "This could be the last day that I'm pregnant."

"I choose to have some faith, Andie. So, I'm not going to play this game with you."

The curtain opened and Dr. Ashford walked in. Ryder moved off the edge of the bed as the doctor washed her hands and pulled gloves out of the box on the table next to the bed.

"When did this start?" Dr. Ashford glanced at the curtain and motioned a tech into the room with a portable ultrasound.

"An hour or so. I woke up and was cramping then."

"Have you been staying down?"

"As much as possible. I had a cow get down today."

"She called me." Ryder shot her a look. "Andie, you walked out into the yard and then back to the house. This isn't your fault."

Dr. Ashford smiled at him and then turned her attention back to Andie. "He's right. Now isn't the time to blame yourself. Now is the time to see what's going on. Any bleeding?"

Ryder stood up. "I'll wait outside."

"No. And, Ryder, stay. I don't want to be alone."

He sat back down. "I'll stay for the ultra-sound."

Dr. Ashford slid a heart monitor over her belly and smiled.

"There's that heartbeat." She paused, frowned and moved it again. "Oh."

"What?" Andie's heart squeezed painfully and she watched, waiting for Dr. Ashford to smile, to say something.

"Let's get that ultrasound in here before I make any big announcements."

Andie leaned, waiting. And praying. Because she needed faith. And she needed God. She wasn't going to believe lies that she was being punished or tossed aside because she wasn't good enough. Old wounds. She tried to tell herself it was time to let them heal. It wasn't easy.

Dr. Ashford squeezed cold gel on her belly and reached for the ultrasound. The tech stood back as the doctor moved the gizmo over her belly, finding the baby, settling on the heartbeat. The doctor nodded and moved the ultrasound a little to the right.

Another heartbeat.

"You're a twin, aren't you?"

"Yes." Her heartbeat was echoing in her ears, beating in unison with the two heartbeats on the ultrasound.

"Andie, you're having twins."

"But there was only one."

"Yes, well, there wasn't only one, but we didn't hear baby number two the last time we checked."

"But they're okay?"

"Andie, they seem to be very okay. I want to do a blood test and keep you here tonight."

"Here, in the hospital?"

"For the night, yes."

Andie's body trembled and she reached for Ryder. His hand tightened around hers.

"Andie, we're having twins." His voice shook a little.

Two babies. Her life had changed, and then

changed again. She looked at Ryder, and to her, he looked a little cornered. And that wasn't what she wanted.

She didn't want him stuck somewhere he didn't want to be, including in a relationship he never planned to have.

Dr Ashford left them alone. She was going to arrange for Andie to have a room for the night, and she thought they might need to catch their breath. She made the last comment with a smile as she walked out the door.

Ryder whistled a lot whistle. "Wow, this it. Not only are we going to do this, but we're going to have twins."

"I'm sorry."

"Why are you apologizing? Andie, we've talked about this. I'm a part of this. I'm the dad. You aren't having a baby, we are having a baby. Two babies."

"Exactly. The guy who didn't want to get married or have kids is now going to have two."

"I know." He sat back in the chair and tried to think about that. "You're going to be on bed rest for a big part of the next seven months."

"Dr. Ashford didn't say that."

"No, but that's the way it works."

"Stop."

He stopped. He knew when a woman was at

the end of the emotional rope swing and about to go off. Andie was dangling.

"We have to get married." He said it with as much conviction as he could, because it was going to take conviction to convince her.

"Excuse me?"

"Married, Andie. We can let Alyson and Jason have their day, but I think we should plan on a Christmas wedding."

"Haven't I already told you no, twice?"

"Yeah, but…"

"But we don't even know yet that the babies are okay. Have you thought of that? Have you thought about putting that ring on my finger and then…"

She could lose the babies.

Of course he hadn't let his thoughts go there. He was a little upset that she would. And he told her so as he stood up.

"Andie, you're emotional. I guess I'm pretty emotional right now, too. But this is crazy. Those babies deserve for us to be married."

"I don't want a proposal that's prefixed with 'this is the right thing to do.' Ryder, just go."

"Go?"

Dr. Ashford walked into the room. "Problem, kids?"

"No, no problem." Ryder grabbed his hat. "Her grandmother will be here in an hour."

"Oh, okay."

As Ryder started his truck, his better self told him to go back and wait. But he couldn't. He was so mad at Andie, he knew he'd say the wrong thing if he stayed. She didn't need that right now. He didn't know what she needed. Definitely not anything he could give.

He'd done his best. He'd proposed three times.

He should have at least stayed to make sure everything was okay after the blood test. But he'd seen the babies, seen their hearts beating. Two of them.

That took a guy some time to adjust to. Two beds. Two ponies. Two frilly pink dresses and two infant carriers in the back of his truck.

Maybe she was right. He wasn't ready for this. He'd been doing the right thing, or what he thought was right, by proposing. But was that really the best thing for them, and for the babies?

Andie was in a darkened hospital room alone when Etta walked through the door, smiling like summer sunshine. Andie looked up, trying to smile back. She'd never felt less like smiling in her life.

She'd chased Ryder out of her room and she was afraid she'd chased him out of her life. But it was for the best. She didn't want him tied to her by guilt.

"Sugar bug, what in the world is going on? I went to the E.R., but they said you'd been moved up here and they didn't know anything."

"Dr. Ashford wants me to stay a night or two, just to keep an eye on the, on the…" she sobbed "…babies."

"Babies?"

"As in two. I was barely adjusting to the idea of one, and now there are going to be two. Two heartbeats, two little babies growing inside me."

"Which explains a lot. Where's Ryder?"

"Home." Andie pushed the button and raised the back of the bed.

"Now, I didn't expect that. He told me he'd wait with you, that he wouldn't think of leaving you alone."

"Yeah, well."

Etta set her yellow purse on the table next to the bed and poured a glass of water that she drank without offering it to Andie. Her lavender-and-gray hair was windblown and her red lipstick was smudged.

"Well, explain to me why Ryder went back on his word. Because Ryder usually keeps his word."

Yes, Ryder did keep his word. And if he

promised to be at her side forever, he'd be there. Even if it wasn't where he wanted to be.

"I told him to leave. I am not going to keep him hooked to my side this way. I'm not going to use this as a way to force him into my life."

"Well now, that's new. I didn't know you wanted him in your life."

"Not like this, I don't. I don't want proposals that start with 'the right thing to do.' I want love." Tears streamed down her cheeks. "I want frilly stinking dresses, fluffy dry cake with jam stuck between the layers and a lot of people crying and wiping their eyes with lace hankies."

"Hormones."

"Probably." Andie took the hankie her granny dug out of her purse.

"You love Ryder. Andie, that's nothing to be ashamed of. It's been as clear as the nose on your face for as long as I can remember. It's just that you've spent a big part of your life playing it safe and pretending you were just his best friend."

Because she kept him in her life that way. The one way to run Ryder off would have been to let him know how she felt. Ryder had always run from females who were looking for forever. He had good reasons, she told herself, even though she knew he was nothing like his dad. He was nothing like his mom.

And now he'd be in her life as the father of

her babies. They'd share weekends. They'd share school pictures. And her heart would break someday when he found someone he loved and wanted in his life forever, someone who got a real proposal.

"Andie, you're going to have to work this out. You're going to have to tell Ryder. Because I'm a pretty good judge of things, and I think he loves you, too. He's just afraid to love anyone."

"I know." She knew about his fears, not about his feelings for her.

"The other thing you have to work out is your relationship with your mother. She called and Alyson told her what is going on. She's flying in tomorrow."

"To help Alyson with the wedding?"

Etta shook her head. "No, to be with you."

Dr. Ashford knocked lightly on the door and stepped into the room. "Etta, did Andie tell you her news?"

"She did. We're so excited."

Dr. Ashford's gaze landed on Andie. "Are we excited?"

"Scared to death is probably more like it." Andie flipped off the TV because it was just noise.

"I think that's probably normal. Andie, a pregnancy like this can be hard on relationships."

Andie shook her head. "There isn't a relationship."

"Oh, there is one, whether the two of you want it or not. You're going to be parents and you're going to start out with double the joy, and double the work. That's a relationship."

"It isn't the end of the world." Etta patted her arm, her smile big, like she meant what she said.

All Andie knew for sure was that she felt sick.

Dr. Ashford touched her arm. "Andie, if you need anything, don't hesitate to call. I know things look a little frightening right now, but I promise you'll adjust. You have months to get used to this. And babies have a way of helping us to grow into parenthood."

"Yes, in most cases." Every single time Andie thought of parenting, she thought about her mother. And she didn't want it that way, with that memory hanging over her head.

Her mother would be there tomorrow. For her. The same woman who walked away, and now she was trying to walk back into Andie's life. She closed her eyes and breathed deep, fighting the sting behind her eyelids as tears tried to push through. She wouldn't cry.

Etta touched her arm and Andie opened her eyes.

"You'll be a good mother. And you're going to have plenty of help." Etta smiled in a way that said she understood.

"Andie, let me know if you need anything." Dr. Ashford patted her foot and walked out the door.

"Alyson is with Jason." Etta sat on the edge of the bed. "She wasn't with me when Ryder called. But I called to tell her what is happening. After that your mother called and Alyson explained the situation to Caroline."

"Call Alyson and tell her she doesn't have to come over. She and Jason have so much to do in the next month."

"I'll tell her, but I can't guarantee she won't come over."

The door opened a few minutes later. Andie's heart jumped a little, expecting it to be Ryder. Because he wouldn't stay gone. He'd never stayed away for long. It wasn't him, of course it wasn't. She had told him to go. It was a nurse's aid with a dinner tray. The young woman set two covered dishes on the table and opened the container of milk.

"Dr. Ashford told me to bring food for you and for your grandmother."

"Thank you." Andie raised her arms and the aid moved the table across the bed.

She was hungry, but she didn't know if she

could eat. Her heart was still breaking, because she hadn't expected to want the person walking through her door to be Ryder. She hadn't expected it to hurt this much when he left.

Etta sat down in the chair next to the bed. She thanked the aid for their food and waited for the young woman to leave.

"Andie, I don't know what is going on with you and Ryder, but I know the two of you will work this out. You'll find a way to be parents to these babies. And I think you'll both do a good job at it."

"I hope you're right."

"Oh, honey, when have I ever been wrong?" Etta winked and then her smile faded. "Goodness gracious, what kind of food is this?"

Andie managed a smile, but it was hard to smile when she didn't know when Ryder would be back. She wouldn't let herself think the worst—that he wouldn't come back.

Chapter Fourteen

Ryder Johnson didn't run. Or at least he'd been telling himself that for the past few days. But it really felt like running. He'd taken his cue from Andie, and he'd run. It wasn't sitting too well with him. He'd called himself things like "yella" and "coward." But it was hard to shake off pretty serious changes to his life, and to Andie's.

He was going to be a dad—to twins. Every single time he thought that, which was often, it felt like a punch to the gut. But it wasn't all bad. He was adjusting. And it was starting to feel a little better, the idea of those two babies in this house.

Since he'd left the hospital, he'd been working on the nursery. The room was painted, all but the trim around the door, and he'd ripped up the carpet. Antique green with antique ivory trim. He didn't get all of these antique colors. His mom had worked hard to make this house look French country and anything but antique.

Ryder stepped back, wanting to see how the room looked from the door, as a first impression. He wasn't very creative, and he wasn't much of a painter, but he thought it looked pretty good. He wondered what Andie would say.

Not for the first time in the past couple of days he thought about calling her. But he wasn't going to push. He'd said what he had to say and now she had to come to terms with things, with life, and with them as parents.

When he left the other day he'd decided they both needed a few days to adjust and think. He had to admit to being knocked on his can with everything that had happened. First the pregnancy, and now twins. He shook his head and looked at the room he had meant for one baby.

Now he thought about how it would be to have the babies here part-time.

He put the brush down and walked around the room, trying to picture it with Andie here, and babies in that crib he was sanding down out in the garage. A room, a crib, a rocking chair and babies. He told himself not to put Andie in this room, not even in his imagination. Babies, yes; Andie, no. But he couldn't stop thinking about her in this room, in this house and in his life.

Floorboards in the hallway creaked. He turned

and Wyatt walked in. He stopped just inside the door and nodded what Ryder hoped was his approval.

"You got it done. I guess that's why you've been up here with the door closed for the past two days." Wyatt wiped a streak of green off the trim at the door.

"Yeah, almost done. Still have to do the trim around the door."

"Word around town is that Andie Forester is having twins."

Ryder hadn't talked to his brother much since the night he came home from the hospital. He'd come home, went out to the barn and knocked around the old punching bag they had in one of the stalls. That was one thing their dad had done for them. He'd taught them to box. He'd given them an outlet. So after his fight with Andie he'd come home and put on boxing gloves.

"Yeah, we're having twins."

"Wow, that's huge."

"Thanks." Ryder put the cap on the paint.

"Is she going to marry you?"

"Nope. She says I have to say something other than 'I think we should.' I'm not sure what she wants from me."

Wyatt laughed, really laughed. "You can't figure it out? You know, everyone in this town thinks you're the ladies' man. But you're really just the guy who dated a lot of women. You know, to be honest, I've never figured out why you didn't date her."

"Because we're friends. I didn't want to mess that up by dating."

Wyatt had said it best; Andie was the longest relationship Ryder had ever had.

But he had messed it up. Instead of dating, he'd taken advantage of her when she needed him the most. He'd done a lot of praying about that, and he'd needed a lot of forgiveness.

"This isn't about protecting your friendship." Wyatt picked up the brush and stroked it across an area that looked smudged. Now that Ryder looked a little closer, maybe it was. He'd never said he was a painter.

"Well then, oh wise one, what do you think it is?" Ryder was about to get those boxing gloves again. It wouldn't be the first time he and Wyatt had settled something in the backyard under the security light.

Wyatt shrugged. "I guess I'd say you're selfish. You didn't want to lose your best friend so you never put yourself out there to see what other kind of relationship you could have with her."

"I asked her to marry me." Ryder growled the words and then he took a deep breath and made his words come out a little quieter. "I asked her to marry me and she said no."

"You asked her like it was a solution to a problem."

"Yeah."

"Yeah? You're an idiot if that's all you can say. You're a clueless idiot and you don't deserve her."

"I'm not clueless… I know exactly what I feel." He stopped, shocked by his own words, and not surprised that Wyatt was smiling.

"Really, what do you feel?"

"I'm not going to hurt her." Ryder looked away from his brother. "I don't want her to be Mom. I don't want to start out thinking we can conquer the world and then someday realize we don't even like each other."

"I guess if you start out thinking someday you'll fail, or things will go south, then you're probably doomed."

"Yeah, I guess we are, but I love her too much to have her hurt that way."

"You love her too much to marry her and be a dad to those babies of yours. Like I said, idiot. You're not our dad. You're the guy who has been in this room for two days, painting it some prissy looking shade of green. You're the guy who has been down in the garage sanding a crib by hand."

Wyatt tossed the brush in the bucket and walked out of the room. Wyatt was getting it together. He'd even taken the girls to church. Ryder would have gone after him but he figured his older brother was figuring out his own life.

He had proposed to Andie by telling her it was the right thing to do. No wonder she was ticked off. And he'd left her in the hospital alone.

It would take a lot of paper to list the mistakes he'd made in his life. And now, at the top of the list was the way he'd treated Andie.

Somehow he'd make it up to her. He'd find a way to show her that he loved her and that he wasn't going to let her down. He wasn't going to be the man who walked away from her. He wasn't going to walk out when things got tough.

But those were words he had to share with her. As soon as he got this room ready. He wanted to show her that he hadn't walked away and forgotten about her. This room was for her.

All this time working up here and he hadn't really thought about it that way. He'd been fixing a room for the babies. That meant having those babies living here, with him. And that meant Andie.

He couldn't picture this room without seeing her in it. And it was that image, man, that image of her, with her blond hair and the sun shining through the window that made him want to have her in this house forever.

Because he loved her. He hadn't ever, not once

in his life, let himself think those words about Andie. But he'd selfishly kept her tied to his side in the place of best friend.

Now he was going to find another way to keep her in his life. And he wasn't going to use the words that had gotten him thrown out of her hospital room.

Andie walked out to the barn. It was great to be able to come and go again. She'd tried not to overdo it, but it had been hard to remember that she still needed to take it easy. She wanted to go everywhere and do everything. She wanted to buy baby clothes in matching sets and pretty pictures for the walls.

The thoughts were pretty out of place in her life. Etta called it nesting and said it would get worse as she got closer to her due date. She shuddered to think about it, about how bad it could get.

She'd had the same bedroom furniture, the same quilt, the same pictures on her walls since as far back as she could remember. And why? Because a girl didn't plan her wedding, or talk about children, when she was in love with her best friend and she knew that he had no intention of ever settling down.

She wondered how much he resented her for taking away his freedom.

Dusty whinnied when he saw her. He trotted up to the fence, his gold coat glimmering in the evening sun. He pushed his head at her, demanding attention and a treat. She pulled baby carrots out of her pocket and held them out to him. He sucked them off her hand, barely moving his lips.

And then she saw the alpaca. She laughed and tears slid down her cheeks. She touched her belly. "That's your dad's idea of romantic."

It wasn't chocolates or roses, although he had brought wilted flowers with the alpaca. But it showed how well he knew her, and how much he cared. He'd bought her an alpaca, a silly thing she wouldn't have bought herself.

"I can't believe he bought you an alpaca." Alyson walked across the yard, pretty and feminine.

Andie tried not to compare herself to her twin. But she did look down at her faded jeans tucked into worn boots. Two peas in a pod, they weren't. But they were connected. Andie should have hunted her sister down. It wasn't fair, that Alyson didn't know about them, but they'd known about her. They should have found her.

But Andie had been too stubborn. She'd decided, without any proof, that Alyson knew about them but didn't want to see them.

She was bad about that assuming thing. She

had assumed, for a lot of years that her mother didn't care about her. She was learning now, since Caroline's arrival the previous day, that maybe more connected them than Andie had thought.

Last night they'd talked about how it felt to be Caroline, leaving her life in the city, trading it for life in Dawson. And then having twin girls.

Last night Andie learned that her mother suffered from chronic depression. And she learned, from her mother, that the biggest difference between them was that Caroline had never felt like a part of Dawson. She had been the wrong fit for Andie's father.

But Andie and Ryder had always been here, always loved their lives here. They knew each other. They knew one another's dreams and goals.

Caroline had helped Andie see that. In a conversation that had been a little stiff, a little formal, Andie had learned about herself from her mother.

"Yeah, an alpaca." She finally answered Alyson's question. "What did you say Jason bought you, a baby grand?"

"Yeah, but Jason knows that I wouldn't have appreciated an alpaca. I think Ryder probably knows how much you'd love one. And you do, right?"

"He's the cutest, sweetest thing in the world."

"The alpaca or Ryder?"

Andie laughed at her sister's very obvious attempt at bringing the conversation back to Ryder. "The alpaca."

"Yeah, of course." Alyson leaned across the fence and scratched Dusty's neck. The alpaca walked toward them, a little slow, hesitant. "How do you feel?"

Andie shrugged. "Good, really. No more cramping. For now, no bed rest. I'm not looking forward to that last trimester. But Dr. Ashford assured me that if I take it easy now, maybe the last trimester won't mean a lot of bed rest."

"That's good to hear. You aren't a good patient."

"Thanks for that." Andie reached to pet the alpaca she'd named George. "I guess I need to try on my dress this week."

"That would be good. The seamstress says she can leave a little room. In case you've gained weight by the end of the month."

"I don't plan on doing that."

Alyson touched Andie's belly. "I have bad news for you. There's a little pooch here now."

"That's water weight."

"Of course it is. But about Ryder…"

"This had to come up, didn't it?" Andie turned

away from the alpaca and they headed toward the house. "Did Etta send you out? She's been after me for three days. Your…our mother has been after me."

"The two of you not talking isn't going to solve anything."

"I never said that I'm not talking to him. He left. He didn't come back." Okay, she'd kind of wanted him to leave at the time, but he didn't have to stay gone.

"Tell him you love him. Give him the opportunity to do the right thing." Alyson said it with such conviction, looping her arm through Andie's as they walked back to the house. "He deserves that honesty from you if you're going to be good parents together."

"Yes, he deserves to know." That she loved him. But once the words were between them, what happened then?

She had no idea. She didn't think it would change anything, though. There were some realities that mattered and wouldn't change. The fact that they were going to have twins was a big reality. He was going to be a dad. She was going to be a mom.

But the two of them together? She wondered if maybe she was being stubborn. She had been called stubborn once or twice. Maybe loving him was enough?

Maybe him loving the babies and being a good husband, being her best friend, was enough? Her heart picked up speed because she'd never felt more like God was showing her something, as if He was really showing her an answer to her prayers for herself and Ryder.

There were starting places in life. Most of those starting places had a lot to do with trusting God, even with a situation that you didn't know how to tackle, or how to face.

"I have to go." She walked through the back door of the house and grabbed her purse off the kitchen table.

"You have to what?" Caroline had walked into the kitchen. Andie paused in the doorway, because it still took her by surprise to see her mother in this house.

"I have to go talk to Ryder."

"Really? Are you done with the silent treatment?"

"I'm done. We have to come to an understanding. I think the understanding is that we're going to be parents and maybe 'I think we should' is a good enough reason to get married. For our babies."

"Oh." Caroline walked to the coffeepot.

"What?"

"Well, I'm glad you're putting the babies ahead of yourself." She poured her coffee and turned.

Andie stood at the door, not sure how to have another conversation with her mother. They'd never discussed the important things in life. They'd barely discussed more than the weather in the three times that they'd met. Except last night, when they'd gotten to know each other a little.

But it still felt like a new pair of boots. She wondered if that would always be their relationship?

Andie guessed probably so if that's all she expected. She breathed a little and let go. Because Caroline wasn't going away anytime soon.

"I love him." Andie slid the strap of her purse over her shoulder and she wondered if her mother saw the parallel between their lives, the way she was seeing it.

"I know you do." But Caroline had never approached anything with faith. Andie was holding fast to hers.

"I know you believe I'm doing the wrong thing. But in my heart I know that going right now and talking to Ryder is the right thing to do. I know that we have to stop being stubborn and be parents."

Caroline smiled. "You're doing the right thing."

Andie nodded and left. She hadn't needed to hear that from her mother, she already knew it.

But it shifted things. A small empty space in her heart closed up a little.

Ryder carried the sanded cradle into the nursery. He planned on painting it that same ivory color. He thought that'd be the right color. First he had to figure out what kind of paint to use. Babies chewed on things. He knew that. Even toddlers chewed on stuff. He'd found Kat chewing on the kitchen cabinet.

He turned at a noise and smiled. Kat was sitting in the doorway, watching. She had a paintbrush and was pretending to paint the door. Fortunately she didn't have paint.

"Good job, Kat."

"Ryder, you have company," Wyatt shouted up the stairs.

Ryder had thought he heard a car come up the drive a few minutes earlier. He brushed his hands down the front of his jeans and wiped dust off his shirt. It might be Andie. Or it might not.

He wondered just how bad a guy could look after getting just a few hours sleep over the last few days. He raked a hand through his hair and hoped for the best. When she came up the stairs, he was waiting for her. Kat was still sitting in the doorway, smiling at her pretend paint job.

"Hi." Andie stopped in the hallway, smiling, looking from him, to Kat, to the open door.

"You look good. I guess it feels good to be out of the house."

"Really good." She shrugged. "It might not last long."

He let his gaze slide to her belly. In a few months he'd be a dad. To twins. Andie was going to be the mother of his kids. And she'd never looked more beautiful. He wanted her to know that.

He took a few steps and when he was close enough, he ran his fingers through her hair, and pulled her closer to him, holding his hand at the back of her neck.

"You look beautiful." He whispered words that he'd never said to her before. And he should have. His teenaged attempts at being cool had included phrases like, "You look hot."

But she was beautiful.

"I'm beautiful?" She blinked a few times and shot a look past him. He turned, smiling at Kat who watched with all of the attention she typically focused on her favorite princess cartoon.

"Yeah, beautiful. I've been meaning to tell you that."

"When you were stumbling over words like, 'Hey, babe, how about you and me get hitched?'"

"I should have told you that you're beautiful

and then said 'Hey, babe, how about if we get hitched.'"

"Not much better." She touched his cheek. "You look beautiful, too."

She stole his breath with those words and that moment. He had too much to say to stop now and hold her the way he wanted to hold her. If he didn't back up he'd never get the words out.

"Ryder, I'm here because I've had time to think, and I want to marry you. I want to raise our babies together." She bit down on her bottom lip. "You don't have to love me, but I love you. I've loved you for as long as I can remember, but I didn't want to lose you by saying something that would push you out of my life."

He hadn't expected that. She could have said almost anything and he'd have been fine, but he hadn't expected love. Or that she'd marry him. And he didn't even have to love her back.

He'd done that to her. All of his macho words about staying single and never falling in love had put these ideas into her mind.

Kat was giggling and she couldn't understand their conversation. He shot her a look and it didn't quell her two-year-old joy an ounce. She was beating on the door, grinning her kind of tooth-less grin.

Ryder turned back to Andie. "That's it, you love me? And now we can get married?"

* * *

Andie hadn't expected that reaction. She swallowed the lump that lodged in her throat. Maybe it was too late for those words. Maybe he'd changed his mind after her third rejection. Not that she blamed him.

And then he smiled. That smile that shifted the smooth planes of his face and took a girl by the heart, holding her tight so she couldn't escape if she wanted to. Andie didn't want to escape that smile or what it did to her heart.

"Andie, I want you to see what I've been doing." He took her by the hand and led her into the bedroom, past the very smiley Kat.

Andie had felt like crying a few times since she'd walked up the stairs and saw Ryder for the first time in three days. But this room, it undid her emotions. Emotions that were raw and close to the surface overflowed when she stood in the center of a room he had planned out and painted.

For their babies. He didn't have to tell her that this was a nursery. The colors and the box of nursery items said it all.

"This is beautiful." She walked around the room, stopping at the rocking chair next to the window. She pictured herself in that chair with her babies.

In this house.

She pictured late night feedings and a lamp glowing softly in the dark. She was holding her babies and Ryder was standing in the doorway, watching. He was leaning against the door frame, his hair a little messy and his feet bare.

She liked him like that. And she liked images of herself in this house.

"Why are you smiling?" Ryder had walked up to her and he leaned in, slipping his arm around her waist and pulling her close.

"I love the room." She touched his shoulder, sliding her hand down to his. "I love you."

He leaned, resting his forehead against hers. "I want you to marry me."

Okay, that was better than his earlier proposals.

"I'll marry you." She swallowed all of her fears, emotions that could become regret and she said it again. "I'll marry you. I want us to raise these babies together, to give them a home where they feel loved and protected."

"What about you?" He was still standing close.

"I'm sorry?"

"What about loving you?"

"You're my best friend."

Ryder reached into his pocket and pulled out the same ring he'd tried to give her three other times. But this time he held onto her hand and sank to one knee. He raised her hand to his lips and kissed her palm. He turned her hand over and slid the ring into place.

"Marry me, Andie. Marry me because I love you so much I can't breathe when you smile at me like that. I want to be more than the father to our babies. And I plan on having a bunch of them. I want to marry you because I love you."

"You love me." She dropped to her knees in front of him and cupped his cheeks in her hands. "You're not just saying that?"

"I'm not just saying that. I love you. It was easy, being your best friend and not worrying about hurting you or losing you. But I love you and I was hurting you. I hurt you by not being honest with you or myself."

"We're both pretty stubborn."

"We are." He lifted her hand and his ring glinted on her finger. He brushed a kiss across her knuckles and then he pulled her close and kissed her again.

Andie closed her eyes, letting her heart go crazy with his words. He held her close and his lips brushed hers again and again and then moved to her ear.

"We have an audience?" He motioned toward the door with his head.

Andie glanced that direction and smiled. Kat

was standing at the door, holding it and watching, her thumb in her mouth.

"That's going to be our lives," she whispered.

"Yeah, I think I'm going to like it a lot."

She was going to like it a lot, too. She was going to love living in this house, being his wife and loving him as he loved her back.

Epilogue

Ryder woke up, wondering why Andie wasn't next to him in bed. It didn't take him long to find her. She was sitting in the rocking chair in the nursery. Her foot was on the cradle in front of her, rocking lightly. But one of his daughters slept in her arms. Both of the girls must have woken up.

He stepped into the room and peeked into the cradle at the sleeping, month old baby girl. Her hair was blond, like her mother's hair. She slept on her side, her fist in her mouth.

The other baby was her identical sister. They were both blond with eyes that might turn brown. Or maybe blue. He'd insisted on matching pink sleepers.

"Which one is eating?" He peeked but couldn't tell.

Andie looked up at him, her features soft in the

dim light of the lamp. She smiled and he would have done anything for her. He would do anything for her. Every moment since she'd married him and moved into his house, their house, had been better because she was part of his life.

And they were a family. In this house they were a family. With Wyatt and the girls in their own place—but always around, at church when they sat on the pew with Etta, Jason and Alyson, they were a family.

"They're your daughters and you can't tell the difference?" she teased.

"No, Mrs. Johnson, I can't. So, who is this?"

She lifted the baby girl and handed her to him. "This is your daughter who needs to be burped while I feed her sister."

He peeked at the tag inside the sleeper. "Ah, my darling Mariah."

"Exactly. And Maggie is about to get her midnight snack."

"This is actually her 3:00 a.m. snack."

He pulled the second rocking chair next to Andie's. That had been a necessity when they'd found out they were having twins. Two rocking chairs. Two cradles. One crib because Andie and Alyson insisted the babies sleep together. And stay together.

These two little girls would never be split up.

They would be protected and they would have parents who raised them with love and security.

Ryder was working hard to keep that promise to his wife and to his little girls.

"I love this room," Andie whispered into the quiet of the room.

"Me, too. I love waking up and having you here. I've never loved this house more than I love it right now."

"Do you know what I love?" Andie shifted her nursing daughter and turned to look at him. "I love looking up and having you standing there, watching me. I dreamed about that the day you proposed. I dreamed of seeing you standing there, your hair messy and your feet bare."

"Really, Mrs. Johnson, I had no idea."

"No, you have no idea." They leaned close together. The kiss was sweet and a promise of something wonderful and lasting.

"I've always loved you, Andie." She cuddled her baby close and smiled, because nothing in the world felt better than being loved by her best friend and knowing that their children would grow up in a family where two parents loved them and they were there for them. Twenty years ago she had pulled petals off a daisy and prayed the last petal would tell her that he loved her. And he did.

* * * * *

Dear Reader,

Welcome back to Dawson, Oklahoma. Andie Forester's story really started with Alyson's story (*THE COWBOY'S COURTSHIP*). It was there that we met the twin sisters and got to know Andie a little bit.

I was excited by the story that unfolded for a heroine who quickly became one of my favorites. I felt like I knew Andie. But as her story unfolded, I realized it wasn't going to be as easy to write as I had assumed.

I didn't undertake this story, or the subject, lightly. I hope that you'll trust me when I say that I prayed about this and labored over the words and how to handle this very delicate subject. People make mistakes. Each of us has done something that we regret, but obviously we can't go back and undo what we've done. So we move forward, we seek God, and we find a way to move forward in grace and with faith.

That's exactly how Andie and Ryder handle their situation. I hope you'll fall in love with these two characters the way I've fallen for them. And come back soon for Wyatt's story.

Many blessings,

Brenda Minton

QUESTIONS FOR DISCUSSION

1. *The Cowboy's Sweetheart* starts with the heroine, Andie Forester, thinking thoughts that are totally foreign to who she believes she is. A situation causes this change. Why do you think she had this change in thinking? What event would, or has caused you, to think differently about your life or situation?

2. Ryder Johnson is afraid to face Andie, but he is there for her because he knows she'll need him. He's also put off by her return to her faith. How difficult would this be for him, to be there and yet have all of these obstacles that would make him want to not be there? What does that say about who he is?

3. Andie's faith isn't really new, it's just a faith that she's returned to. Why would facing her mother be the last thing she wanted to do at that moment?

4. Andie and Ryder made a promise to keep boundaries between them. Would it have been better, and easier, for them to face life and their feelings honestly and take each situation as it came to them?

5. Andie and Ryder made a mistake/choice that resulted in consequences that are life-long. How can we distinguish between consequences and discipline? Is there a big distinction?

6. The Bible says that the Lord disciplines those whom He loves. Andie had the idea that God was out to punish her, or hurt her, for her actions. Is this wrong or right thinking?

7. Ryder proposed to Andie believing it was the "right thing to do." Why would that proposal be the wrong thing to do? How could it be right?

8. When faced with the possibility of a miscarriage, Andie's thoughts about the baby changed. How?

9. Losing her independence wasn't easy for Andie. Her faith was tested, but Ryder found more strength. Is it normal, for faith to have highs and lows? How does it help us to have someone with stronger faith to encourage us during those times?

10. Ryder is determined to marry Andie, even though he's struggling with the romance part

of the equation. When does he finally get it right?

11. How does the idea of being a parent change Ryder?

12. When does Ryder really figure out that he loves Andie and has probably loved her for a long time? Do you think he always knew but was afraid of hurting her, or was it a moment when he fell in love with her?

13. Life changes. Andie and Ryder were living very single, individual lives. One moment, one choice changed all of that. They went from single, to having a baby, to possibly losing that baby, and then having twins. How do changes in life change us? How does it change our faith?

14. People with faith have values that they live by, according to God's word. We try to be who God wants us to be, but sometimes we fail. We make choices with long lasting consequences. Andie and Ryder made a choice and that choice changed their lives. In the end they found happiness and faith, but was it easy to deal with the consequences of their actions?

LARGER-PRINT BOOKS!

**GET 2 FREE
LARGER-PRINT NOVELS
PLUS 2 FREE
MYSTERY GIFTS**

Love Inspired®

Larger-print novels are now available...

LILP10R